The passionate kiss disturbed them both

Nick looked from her eyes to her mouth, convulsively swallowed and looked away.

"When Peter was killed I told myself that I'd make you pay for what you did to him," he said hoarsely.

She opened her lips to deny, but the burning blue eyes ripped through her.

"No, you listen to me. It was a mistake to let me see you wanted me, Caroline. You handed me my weapon on a plate...."

Caroline's body stiffened, the skin on the back of her neck prickling.

"You'll stay here in my house, where I can keep an eye on you. No more men. No affairs. You're going to pay and pay in your own coin. I'm going to make you suffer the way Peter suffered."

CHARLOTTE LAMB

heartbreaker

Harlequin Books

TORONTO • LONDON • LOS ANGELES • AMSTERDAM
SYDNEY • HAMBURG • PARIS • STOCKHOLM • ATHENS • TOKYO

Harlequin Presents edition published October 1981
ISBN 0-373-10460-X

Original hardcover edition published in 1981
by Mills & Boon Limited

CHAPTER ONE

THE COMEDY SHOW was boring her back teeth out, but she was too tired to get up and switch off the set. A door slammed somewhere, and Caroline tensed. Kelly? Had she woken up and gone to the bathroom? There had been a period a while back when Kelly had sleepwalked. Caroline had been terrified; she hadn't dared wake her up. She had hovered around her until Kelly marched back into bed, then she had cried helplessly, wondering what buried memories were making her daughter wander around the house like a lost soul.

That had stopped in time, though, thank God. Kelly hadn't walked in her sleep for nearly a year. Children had tougher minds than you thought. They got over things that left scars on more adult skin.

Getting up, Caroline switched off the TV set. She went out of the room, but everything in the little bungalow was quiet. Kelly's door was closed. There wasn't a sound from her.

I must have imagined it, thought Caroline. *Three years and I'm still scared out of my wits.* Would it always be the same? She pushed fear to the back of her mind, but in that dark cupboard it germinated and put out horrible pale roots that snaked up through the levels of consciousness to disturb her when she least expected it.

She was about to go back into the lounge when she heard the footsteps on the path. The doorbell sounded, and she jumped. Deirdre? She often popped round in the evening to borrow a cup of sugar or tell Caroline some fascinating anecdote about the milkman.

Opening the door, Caroline had a smile ready. The wind whipped past her, blowing her soft honey-blond curls into a frothy tangle, and she pushed them away from her face with one hand, beginning to laugh.

The laughter cut out as the light from the hall behind her fell onto a powerful frowning face. Cuttingly cold blue eyes held her startled gaze. In a reflex action she gasped and tried to slam the door shut again. It was shoved wide open, the man's shoulders thrusting it back so violently that Caroline was flung backward. Her shocked cry of alarm was muffled by one hand. The door closed with the man on the same side as she was.

She pressed against the wall, her face white, her green eyes huge, her heart hammering against her breastbone.

"Hello, Caroline," he said, and the deep icy voice was exactly the same, although she hadn't heard it for three years.

She had only half her attention on him. She was listening for other footsteps, another voice, because if *he* was here she knew Kelly was going to hear him. Her mind whirled in a fog of confusion and fear. She moistened her dry lips with the tip of her tongue, swallowing on the hard knot of terror in her throat.

"What are *you* doing here?"

It had to come out, a strangled question that left out so much that it was almost meaningless. "Are you alone?"

The blue eyes narrowed contemptuously as they watched her. The straight hard mouth compressed.

"Yes, I'm alone." He did not ask what she meant, of course. He did not show any surprise at the question.

The intensity of fear slackened slightly, but it was only a postponement, a deferring of the inevitable, and she still stood rigidly against the wall, watching him with dilated pupils that made her skin seem even more translucent, bloodless.

"What do you want?" Caroline whispered, but that was not what she wanted to ask; it was not what was occupying her mind.

His smile flickered derisively, because of course he understood all that she had left unasked, unspoken, and Caroline became angry as she met his cold stare.

"How did you find me?"

"A private detective," he drawled, and Caroline was sickened by the idea of someone trailing her, asking questions, watching her while she was unaware of prying eyes.

"It took him a long time," he said. "You were clever. You covered your tracks very well, but then you meant to, didn't you? You had no intention of being found."

"How did he find me?" she asked, because she couldn't imagine how he had, unless her solicitor had betrayed her, and he had promised he wouldn't give her address to anyone. That had been the only stray thread left dangling—unavoidably.

He smiled. "I've no intention of telling you," he taunted, then took off the heavy black overcoat he was wearing and tossed it onto a chair in the little hall with a casual movement.

Caroline was dry mouthed suddenly. She looked away so that she would not stare too hard at the ripple of muscles under the expensive pin-striped suit, the cool cutting edge of his profile, the thick black eyelashes that drooped against his cheek as he glanced around him. She had defenses against everything but herself.

"Aren't you going to ask me in?" he demanded, and she looked back at him but did not quite meet his eyes because she was afraid he might glimpse something she did not want him to see.

"You seem to be in, without any invitation."

She felt rather than saw his cool smile. "You were hardly welcoming."

Caroline didn't bother to answer that.

"I'm not accustomed to having doors slammed in my face," he murmured in a light voice that did not hide the anger underlying it.

He made the little hall look smaller than ever as he moved away, raking back his thick black hair with one hand. Nick Holt was a physically overpowering man: wide shouldered, very tall, his body lean and tapering and very fit. She remembered only too vividly that when he was relaxed and at ease he could be charming, the hard force of his nature softened by the teasing smile those blue eyes could hold, but she knew she was not going to glimpse any of his charm tonight. Nick had not smiled at her like that for years. He had stopped long before she and Kelly fled.

"This place belongs to you—you've bought it?" he asked, but the question had a rhetorical ring, because no doubt he already knew the answer. How much information had his detective dug up about her?

"Yes," she answered, because forcing herself to speak quietly and calmly helped her to feel as if she were in command of herself.

He strolled into the lounge and stood looking around in open curiosity. It was not a large room, but it had an open, uncluttered look, largely because Caroline hadn't been able to afford to do more than furnish it with the bare minimum of necessities. The carpet had been bought in a sale, and the three-piece suite had been bought on a discount from a firm whose publicity her agency handled. She had put up the wallpaper and painted the woodwork herself. It was amazing what you could do when you put your mind to it. During the past three years Caroline had discovered abilities and strengths within herself that she had never suspected.

There was a large, unframed childish painting on one wall. Nick Holt crossed over to look at it while she watched him anxiously. Kelly had painted it a year ago. It was of a house with black windows and had been done with explosive force, considering Kelly had been only six when she painted it. A shadow fell from the house across the garden, reaching out toward two tiny running figures.

Caroline had been sick when she first saw the painting. Kelly's teacher had taken her aside to show it to her, her face disturbed. They had both recognized that in putting her feelings down on the paper, Kelly was working things out in her own way, bringing her anxieties out into the open, and Caroline had put the picture up on the wall so that it stayed in the open, right where they could both see it and face it. Perhaps that had freed Kelly of the dark memories at last, because soon after painting it she had stopped walking in her sleep.

It made Caroline nervous now to have Nick Holt look at Kelly's painting. She broke into stammered speech to distract him.

"What are you doing here? Why have you come?"

"Why do you think?" He swung around and surveyed her, his face harsh.

"Look, I don't want to be rude," Caroline said nervously. "But I don't want to talk; there's nothing to say."

"I'll do the talking," he told her, his voice chipped with ice.

"Please," she broke out, and he pushed his hands into his pockets and watched her with that hostile face.

"I'm not leaving until I've said what I came to say. I've come a long way to see you, and now that I'm here you are going to listen."

A little false courage seeped into her. She moved to the door, saying, "I'm afraid I must insist."

He didn't move. He just watched her with that tight smile and dislike in his blue eyes.

"My neighbors can hear every sound," she said warningly. "One scream and they would be here to find out what was going on."

He was beside her before she had finished the sentence. Those long legs of his could cover the ground like greased lightning. As her lips parted on a scream, his hand clamped over them. She stared at him over the muffling fingers, making a muffled protest.

"Scream away." He was smiling, but it was a very grim smile, without humor, and it did not lighten the atmosphere between them.

The proximity of that lean body had caused a quiver of pain and disturbance to pass over her. She looked away, her eyes flickering past him, the gold-tipped lashes cloaking them to hide her expression; but he was watching her very closely, and he could feel the odd softness of the mouth silenced by his fingers.

Neither of them moved or spoke. The sound of their mingled breathing seemed to fill the little room. Caroline was trembling violently. The emotion inside her was no longer fear. An intensity of awareness gripped her by the throat.

She heard Nick draw a sharp breath. He released her and swung away. She couldn't stay on her feet. She sat down before she fell, sinking onto the small couch and letting her head bend forward slightly because she was afraid she was going to pass out. Her body was wrapped in ice.

As if Nick, too, needed a moment to recover, he walked around the room, touching things, staring at what he saw. Caroline was waiting for her breathing to slow down, her heart to stop shuddering convulsively inside her chest.

When the turmoil did subside she began to think again and to realize that from now on she wasn't safe here. Her fortress had been breached; her security was gone, her cover blown. She was going to have to run again and take Kelly out of the reach of that black shadow.

It had been such a struggle to build up the life they had now. Caroline did not know where she was going to find the courage to start all over again. Just to consider it made her tired.

"Helen's been very ill," Nick said abruptly, swinging around to face her.

Her heart stopped again for a brief moment. Sickness churned in her stomach.

"Ill?" she repeated, searching Nick's face with terrified eyes but not finding any answers in it. Surely he hadn't turned on Helen? What had happened?

"Pneumonia," he said.

In a mixture of relief and distress, Caroline repeated, "Pneumonia?"

"She nearly died. We thought she had had it, but then she miraculously pulled through. She's still very weak, though. And she wants to see Kelly."

Caroline's heart ached. It could be a trap, a lie, but she didn't think it was. His face had a somber cast to it. Caroline loved Helen; she longed to see her again. But she shook her head, her lips trembling.

"I'm sorry, I wish I could agree."

"You not only can, you will," Nick interrupted, a flare of angry color invading his face. "I've promised Helen I'll bring her granddaughter home and I intend to keep my promise."

His voice had risen too loudly. She looked at the door, flinching. "Keep your voice down. These walls are as thin as paper. Do you want to wake her up?"

The last thing in the world she wanted was for Kelly to wake up, come in here, see him.

He turned away on a tense, irritated movement and strode across the room. There was a large studio portrait of Kelly on the polished teak sideboard. Nick picked it up and stared at it for a long moment.

"She's nothing like you, is she?" Kelly had a heart-shaped little face that was cute rather than pretty. Her skin was olive, and her amber eyes perfectly matched the glossy brown bell of her straight hair.

"No," Caroline agreed. She hesitated, then said huskily, "She has the look of Helen sometimes."

He shot her a glance from under those thick black lashes. "Yes, I thought that." He put the photograph down. "When was it taken? Is it recent?"

"Yes, it was done six months ago at school." Every year a local photographer visited the school and took both group and individual photographs of the children that the parents could then buy at a special price. Caroline couldn't have afforded a session in the photographer's studio, but she had been delighted with the picture he had taken at the start of the spring term, and she had had this one framed.

"She looks well," Nick said. "She was always a little pale as a baby, I seem to remember."

Caroline looked away. Oh, yes, Kelly had been pale. Children have antennae that pick up the emotions of those around them, even if those emotions are hidden. Even in her pram Kelly had known, the big brown eyes faintly worried as they gazed up at her mother. A small child shouldn't be so highly strung that she flinches at every little noise, but Kelly had been. She had been painfully quiet. People had often said to Caroline, "What a good baby; she hardly makes a sound," but Caroline had not thought that was a matter for congratulation. Kelly had been unnaturally quiet, careful to keep a low profile, wary and hypersensitive.

She was not like that now. In the past three years Kelly had gradually relaxed. She laughed naturally now. She was high-spirited and lively, a normal, noisy seven-year-old who did not keep looking over her shoulder with a nervous frown every five minutes. Kelly was happy and confident at last, and she was not ever going to be frightened again if Caroline could help it.

"Nick," she said quietly, "I can't explain, but I can't bring Kelly back to Skeldale, not even for Helen...."

He looked at her harshly, with biting contempt, because he despised and condemned her, and she couldn't defend herself.

"Peter's dead," he said, and she stared at him blankly while the words fell through her mind heavily, like stones, crashing through layers of understanding, feeling, reaction, without any of it showing on her white face.

Although she was staring at Nick she was not seeing him, and the emptiness of her large green eyes betrayed that. Her mind was shell-shocked, dazed, grasping for some reality in the face of the news because she'd been left limp and weak by the awful slackening of a fear that had held her for years.

Nick's voice thickened and hardened, and there was

anger in his blue eyes as he watched her. He flung words at her as if he were trying to batter some reaction out of her.

"He crashed his car three months ago and was killed outright; drove straight into a parked lorry and turned his car into a heap of old junk."

She was trembling, her hands locked together in her lap, her blank eyes fixed on him while she listened.

He moved restlessly, his face violent with rage. "My God, you're a cold-blooded little bitch! Can't you even pretend to be sorry? I tell you that your husband is dead and you just sit there like a statue and don't say a damned word. No tears, no regret, not even a bloody question. What sort of woman are you? He was your husband for five years. Doesn't that mean a thing to you?"

He had pierced the brittle shell of her self-defense, his brutal voice shattering it. In an instinctive childish gesture, Caroline put her hands over her eyes to hide her face from him, and he bent down to wrench away her fingers, taking hold of her chin and forcing her head back so that he could glare down into her eyes.

"Don't try to hide your face from me," he snarled, and tears welled into the big green eyes as they met his stare. He swore under his breath as he watched them trickle from under her drooping lashes. His fingers tightened on the rounded curve of her chin, then he flung her face away with a bitter gesture and turned on his heel, stalking toward the fireplace.

"And you can stop the crocodile tears," he bit out. "They're too late and they don't work with me, Caroline."

She brushed a trembling hand over her wet eyes, fighting to regain control. Now that the first shock had passed she was being swamped by waves of emotions he would not understand and she could never confide to him.

Nick stood staring at the floral pattern on the carpet, his toe tracing the curving green tendrils woven between the pink flowers.

When her voice seemed to be back under control, Caroline asked huskily, "How did Helen take it?"

"Hard," he said without looking up, and she could imagine it. Helen would have felt the same terrible mingling of shock and relief that had just knocked Caroline off balance, but Nick wouldn't know that. She knew he still had no idea from the way he spoke to her, looked at her. Helen had kept her secrets.

Oh, poor Helen, she thought miserably. *What must she have gone through? And I wasn't there. I'm the only person in the world who understands what Helen has been feeling, the only one she could have talked to honestly, knowing I would listen without shock or questions. She must have had to shut it all inside her, pretend, go on with the bitter charade she has been playing for years.*

Nick's blue eyes were on her face again, their coldness even deeper.

"She's never been the same since. I wasn't surprised when she got pneumonia. She had been heading for trouble for weeks. She wasn't looking after herself. She didn't eat, didn't go out; she lost so much weight she looked like a scarecrow. I think she wanted to die. It's surprising she pulled through the pneumonia. She didn't have the strength of a mouse. Somehow they kept her alive, and I want her to stay alive. That's why I'm here. That's why you're coming back with me, you and Kelly, if I have to drag you bodily."

She nodded. There was no longer any reason why she shouldn't go back.

His mouth twisted in an unpleasant little smile. "Do I take it that you'll come?"

"Yes," she said.

"You've changed your tune," Nick said, and walked away in that restless angry way toward the wall. "But then we both know why, don't we?" He swung around, his voice rising again. "I knew that when I told you Peter was dead you'd change your mind!"

In the silence that followed, the telephone rang, and they both looked at it in startled surprise.

Caroline shakily got up and went to answer it. "Caroline? Are you okay?" Deirdre sounded half worried, half sheepish. "I don't want to be nosy, but I thought I heard a man shouting in there. Is everything all right?"

"Yes. I've got a visitor, that's all." Caroline tried to sound normal, injecting a slight smile into her voice. "Family problems—someone has been ill. Thanks for ringing; I appreciate it."

Deirdre groaned. "Robin said I was being silly, but knowing you're on your own I just had to make sure nothing was wrong."

"I'm very grateful; it was nice of you."

"Robin said it was probably Grey." There was the faintest question mark in that remark, because of course Deirdre was dying of curiosity.

"No," Caroline said. "It isn't him."

She felt Nick move behind her and glanced at him. He was standing a few feet away, his hands in his pockets, his face hard.

"I'll have to go away," Caroline said. "For a few days."

"Would you like me to have Kelly for a while?" Deirdre was always ready to baby-sit for her. She had a daughter the same age as Kelly, and the two little girls were as close as twins. They did everything together.

"Oh, that's very kind of you, but she will be going with me. We're going to visit her grandmother."

"Oh," Deirdre said, surprised because Caroline had never breathed a word about having any relatives. Indeed, she had deliberately given the impression that she hadn't a living soul in the world but Kelly.

"Okay," Deirdre said when Caroline proffered no further information. "Look, I'll come round tomorrow morning early and check if there's anything you want me to do, okay?"

"Thank you, that's good of you," Caroline said, and then Deirdre said good-night and rang off.

Caroline replaced the receiver and turned to find Nick watching her with antagonism in his face. She tried to hide her involuntary flinch, but he saw it and his mouth tightened.

"Who was that?" His voice was deep and harsh.

"My next-door neighbor. She heard you shouting." Caroline gave him a bitter little smile. "I told you that my neighbors can hear every little noise."

"That must make life difficult for you at times," he said, the icy blue eyes stripping her.

If she had missed the stinging implication behind the words, she would have known they were intended to be unpleasant by the faint curl of his mouth as he spoke. She had no intention of allowing him to see that he had got that dig home. She looked at him blankly.

His face stiffened again. "I drove down here from Skeldale," he said. "I'll drive you and Kelly back with me."

"Thank you," she said dryly.

There was a long silence while he stood there, the frown darkening his features, his hands in his pockets.

"Helen knows you've found me?" she asked huskily.

He looked at her, his mouth curling at the edges again. "Not yet."

That surprised her. Why hadn't he told Helen?

"I decided to wait until I'd seen you for myself," Nick said. "I didn't know what I'd find."

"Your private detective didn't tell you much?" There was irony in her expression as she asked that, and Nick's cold eyes flicked over her in response to her tone.

"He told me all he could discover. I wasn't sure it was all there was to know."

"What else were you expecting?"

"Why are you alone?" he asked in a flat hard voice, and she stared at him blankly.

"Alone?"

"Here, just you and Kelly. What happened to Stephen Ryland?"

Caroline was totally adrift. What on earth was he talking about? "Stephen Ryland?" she repeated, her eyes fixed on him.

The coldness in his face was replaced by a blinding flash of rage that made her inwardly leap back, her body growing rigid, although she did not move.

"Don't pretend you don't know what I'm talking about! It wasn't hard to put two and two together. You left Skeldale the same day as Ryland, and Peter already had suspicions of what was going on between the two of you."

So that was it, she thought wryly. That was how Peter had explained her sudden flight.

"I didn't even know Stephen had left Skeldale," she said in a quiet voice.

"You didn't know?" Nick mocked. "My God, if I didn't know better I'd almost believe you. Those big green eyes are deceptively innocent. What happened? Did he run out on you? Or was it the other way around? Got tired of him, did you?"

She looked at him wearily, her face pale. "Would you believe me if I told you that I haven't set eyes on Stephen Ryland since I left Skeldale, that I didn't know he had left, too, and have no interest in him whatever?"

"No, I wouldn't believe you," he said dryly.

Her shoulders moved in a sigh. "No," she said. What else had she expected? Nick had swallowed everything Peter had ever told him and he wasn't going to listen to her, especially as she couldn't tell him the truth even now.

"How have you been living?" Nick asked. "How did you get this place? It must have cost quite a bit." He looked around the room again, his brows rising with sardonic dismissal. "It's a little like a rabbit hutch to look at from outside, but I suppose in London it is quite a desirable residence.''

A little red spot showed in each of her cheeks. "My father died four years ago and by the time the Australian lawyers had sorted out his estate I found myself with quite a large sum of money." It had taken every penny of her father's legacy to help to buy the bungalow, though, and she only just managed to pay the taxes and bills and feed herself and Kelly on her salary.

"Handy," Nick murmured dryly, and she frowned. It was true—she would never have been able to support herself and Kelly three years ago when she left Skeldale if she hadn't had that money from her father. The legacy had come at precisely the right moment and it had saved her sanity, if not Kelly's life.

"How do you manage to hold down a full-time job at a big advertising agency and look after Kelly?" he asked.

"My next-door neighbor takes Kelly to school and fetches her again in the afternoon. Her daughter is in Kelly's class. Kelly stays with them until I get back in the evening. Deirdre has been marvelous; I don't know what I would have done without her."

Nick's mouth held dry mockery. "So she gets landed with Kelly while you go out to work?"

She stiffened angrily. "I don't impose on Deirdre, if that's what you're implying! The arrangement suits us both."

"I'm sure it does," he drawled, and his eyes told her that he didn't believe a word of it.

"Deirdre likes earning extra money without having to go out to work to get it. It gives her a little income of her own, makes her feel more independent.'' Deirdre had worked in a large department store before she married and the only job she could get around here was something of that sort, which she didn't want to do.

"I pay her by the hour," Caroline said fiercely, "and at the going rate for baby-sitting around here. I don't take advantage of her."

She was all the more angry because she couldn't help feeling guilty about the way she and Kelly lived, although she knew she had no choice. She had to work, and her job paid very well. They needed the money she could earn at the agency, but all the same, Caroline couldn't shake off her worry and guilt about the hours she spent away from her daughter.

She looked with dislike at Nick's hard ironic face. What did it matter what he thought? She had enough trouble coping with her own emotional problems; she wasn't going to let Nick Holt undermine her.

"Would you mind going now?" she asked him, turning away. "I'm very tired. What time will you pick us up tomorrow?"

"Nine," he said, following her into the hall. She watched him pick up his overcoat and shrug into it, pushing back his thick black hair with one hand as he straightened the collar.

"Good night," he said, and then his eyes roamed down over her in a sexual appraisal meant to leave her in no doubt as to what he thought of her, his cold eyes following the line of the small high breasts, slim waist and curved hips that the figure-hugging pink woolen dress suggested more revealingly than she would have liked at this moment.

Caroline's color surged up into her face. The green eyes flashed angrily at him as he opened the front door.

"Sweet dreams," Nick murmured mockingly. Then the door slammed and he was gone, and she broke into scalding, helpless floods of tears.

CHAPTER TWO

HER DOCTOR had prescribed some sleeping pills for her several years ago, but she had been scared to take them in case she slept too deeply and didn't hear Kelly calling for her. She hadn't slept well for years, and some nights she got hardly any sleep at all. It was surprising how little sleep you could manage on. She had got used to five or six hours and could manage on four if she had to.

Tonight she fell asleep almost the minute her head touched the pillow. She had cried for an hour before she went into her bedroom, after first looking in on Kelly. The little girl had been sleeping in that deep, deep sleep of childhood, her face sideways on her pillow, one arm flung up above her brown hair. Caroline had gently placed Kelly's arm under the bedclothes and kissed her forehead before she tiptoed out again.

When she woke up the birds were singing in the garden. She had forgotten to set the alarm, but when she looked at the clock it was only just gone seven and she had plenty of time.

She lay watching the autumn sunlight trickle around the room and realized with a shock that very soon she would be in Skeldale. The name brought back a piercing flood of memories: springy purple heather, blue autumn skies, the gleam of slate roofs in sunlight.

She heard Kelly moving about and tensed. She was going to have to tell her, but how was she to break the news? The prospect made her feel sick. Kelly was quite mature for a child of her age, but death was not something a child would understand, and Caroline was afraid of her daughter's reaction.

The door opened and her daughter's reproachful, half-gleeful face stared at her across the room. "It's nearly half-past seven; you didn't get up. We'll be late."

Caroline held out her hand, smiling nervously. "You're not going to school today, darling. Come here. I want to talk to you."

Kelly climbed into the bed and snuggled down in the warmth. "It isn't Saturday," she said doubtfully.

"I've got something to tell you," Caroline said, and Kelly looked worried. Children, like animals, have instincts beyond their understanding. Kelly was picking up the nervous vibrations of her mother's mood, and she didn't like it.

"It's daddy," Caroline said, and felt the immediate stiffening of the little body.

Telling Kelly was one of the hardest things Caroline had ever had to face, and she would have picked a better moment if she'd had time, but she knew she would have to do it before Nick arrived—before they set off for Skeldale.

Kelly's reaction was oddly similar to her own, and although the little girl cried, Caroline understood that she was guilty and frightened because she, too, could not mourn for Peter; she could only feel relief and a falling away of fear. Kelly might not have wished her father dead, but she had wished him away, had been terrified of him, and now she was full of guilt and misery.

"Daddy was sick, darling," Caroline told her. "He was very sick, and you mustn't blame yourself."

It was good for Kelly to cry, though. Tears would wash away the hard stone of guilt and let out all the buried feelings of hostility and fear, those emotions that had given such a powerful charge to the painting of the darkened house and garden.

Caroline lifted her out of bed. "We're going to see grandma," she told her. "You want to see your grandma, don't you? We're going today, so we must get a move on, mustn't we? You have a wash while I get breakfast for you."

"Grandma?" Kelly asked, her tears slackening. "Are we really? Are we going to Skeldale?"

"Of course to Skeldale—where else would we see grandma?" Caroline rushed her into the bathroom and patted her on the bottom. "Now, miss, wash properly and then get dressed."

She heard Kelly tumbling down the corridor as she put the boiled egg into the fat yellow eggcup and covered it with the little chicken cozy that she had knitted for it. She knitted all Kelly's sweaters; it was a comforting way of keeping busy while she watched television in the long evenings.

Kelly came quietly into the room and sat down, her face still pale, looking painfully adult as she stared at the food Caroline put in front of her.

"I'm not hungry, mummy."

"Try to eat something. It is a long drive."

Kelly looked up. "Drive? Are we going in a car?"

Caroline nodded. "Uncle Nick is taking us. Do you remember him?"

Kelly frowned. "Isn't he... wasn't he daddy's cousin, mummy? He lived in Skeldale."

"That's right, and he will be picking us up in about an hour, so while I pack a suitcase and get dressed, why don't you eat your breakfast? Would you like some cold milk?"

Kelly nodded and began slowly to eat her cereal, her mouth turning down at the edges a little.

Deirdre knocked at the back door and came into the room, looking at Caroline with friendly concern. "Everything okay?"

Caroline nodded. "I don't know how long we'll be away. Could you tell the headmistress that Kelly will be away for a while?"

"Yes, of course."

"And could you cancel the milk and papers?" Caroline searched her mind for anything else she should remember.

"I've got my key. I'll let myself in and check that everything is okay," Deirdre promised. "Don't worry about anything. Leave a phone number and if anything goes wrong I'll get in touch."

Caroline didn't have to look up Helen's phone number; she knew it all too well. She scribbled it down and handed it to Deirdre.

"Anything else?" Deirdre asked.

"If you had a moment, I'd be grateful if you could water my pot plants. They ought to be watered about twice a week."

"Right. Anything else?" Deirdre was poised on one

foot. She had to get back to Sharon, of course, who would also be eating her breakfast at this moment.

"No, I don't think so." Caroline smiled at her. "You don't know how grateful I am. Thanks. I'll do the same for you one day."

"Look after yourself and keep in touch," Deirdre said, then smiled at Kelly. "Have a nice trip, Kelly."

Kelly said, "Say bye to Sharon for me," and Caroline was afraid she would start crying again, but she didn't, although her lower lip was trembling.

"Well, bye," Deirdre said as she left, and Caroline flew into the bathroom. When she was dressed she packed a case for herself and for Kelly. Kelly went through clothes at an alarming rate; she seemed to attract dirt like a magnet.

That done, she rang Grey, and he was extremely scathing. "How long will you be away? What am I supposed to do in the meantime?" Grey was a gifted publicist. He had a mind that thought in slogans, a smooth bland face that had the capacity to take on any expression it chose and be entirely convincing, and a tongue like a razor.

"I'm sorry, but it can't be helped," she said. She had never discussed her marriage with him, but she thought he guessed something of what she had never told him. Grey's intuition was keen and the mind behind the very bright hazel eyes was shrewd and sophisticated.

Kelly was washing up her breakfast things when her mother came into the kitchen. The table was clear, and Kelly carefully placed her cereal bowl in the plastic drainer as Caroline watched her.

"Good girl." Kelly had learned to help around the

house, especially in the morning rush before they both went off to work and school.

The doorbell sounded. Kelly jumped.

"That must be Uncle Nick," said Caroline brightly, hoping her own apprehension was not showing in her face. "Why don't you go and let him in, darling?"

Kelly went out of the room slowly. Caroline heard the front door open and Nick said, "Hello, you must be Kelly. You've changed beyond all recognition. Aren't you tall!"

He never used that warm gentle voice to *her*, thought Caroline. She went out as Kelly was answering him, and Nick looked at her briefly, his hard face unsmiling.

"Are these your cases? I'll put them in the car."

"Thank you." They were being very polite to each other in Kelly's presence. Nick picked up the cases and went out with them and Caroline zipped Kelly into her fur-lined anorak, her fingers not quite steady.

"I do remember him now," Kelly said, excitement in her voice. "He's nice."

"Go to the bathroom before we leave," Caroline said, ignoring that.

"I've just been," Kelly insisted, dancing about.

Before Caroline could stop her, she had darted out. Caroline put on her own coat and buttoned it with faintly shaky fingers. Only now did she stop to realize that for the next few hours she was going to be sitting in a car with Nick. She would share the back with Kelly; it would avoid the nervous tension of the proximity to him.

She closed the front door and went out. The sunlight made the wooded prospect below the hill look inviting.

At night you could see the lights of other houses like a thousand stars at the foot of the hill, but this morning the whole sky lay blue and open as far as the eye could see, London stretching away on the horizon, a huddled mass of roofs, spires, tower blocks. The suburb lay on the outer perimeter of the city, eight miles from the center. London sprawled in a great gray circle, growing every day, eating up acres of green countryside and little villages.

Caroline took a deep breath. Her memories of Skeldale were so troubled that they had quite wiped out the beauty of the little Yorkshire town with its surrounding moorland. How would it feel to be going back there and to know that the shadow no longer lay over it?

She walked to the waiting car. Typical of Nick Holt: it was a sleek black Porsche. While she stared at it in fascinated admiration, Nick took her elbow and pushed her into the seat beside him. Kelly was curled up in the back seat behind her.

"What a super car! Isn't it a super car, mummy?"

"Super," Caroline said wryly as Nick got in beside her.

He gave her a sardonic glance as he started the engine. The powerful roar quieted to a hushed throb as they moved away.

Caroline looked over her shoulder and saw Deirdre standing on the path outside her bungalow, a coat flung around her, staring after the Porsche with fascinated curiosity. Caroline waved and Deirdre waved back.

"We should make Skeldale by lunch," Nick murmured, taking the corner smoothly.

"How fast can it go?" Kelly demanded, leaning forward, her nose between them and an excited flush on her face.

Caroline glanced at the little girl anxiously. The news about her father seemed to have been pushed to the back of her mind, but children were so deceptive. Kelly had learned to suppress unpleasant memories, and you can never entirely suppress anything. For the moment, though, Kelly was absorbed in the excitement of going back to Skeldale in the fast, sleek car. She had never been in a car like this—and neither had Caroline. It was a first for both of them.

"Wait until we hit the motorway and I'll show you," Nick promised, and Caroline's heart sank. She did not like fast cars.

"Wow!" Kelly said on a reverent note, and she looked at Nick with shiny adoring eyes. Caroline glanced away, frowning.

She listened as Nick talked to her daughter in a relaxed and casual way that was not patronizing but which did not run too far ahead of the child's ability to respond to what he said. Kelly was breathless with enjoyment. Caroline did not need to see her face to know that Nick had knocked her cold. Kelly had never seen anyone like him. He was even more breathtaking than Wonderwoman.

Once they were on the motorway heading northward, the Porsche soared away and other drivers stared enviously after them as they passed slower cars. Caroline watched out of the corner of her eye as Nick's long powerful fingers effortlessly manipulated the wheel. Looking away, she swallowed. She hated herself for that insidious drag of the senses, the dangerous awareness of him that she had been forced to recognize during the last year before she left Skeldale.

Nick had not missed the few signals she had unwarily betrayed back then. Once or twice he had caught her looking at him, and it was then that those fierce blue eyes had begun to hold distaste and hostility.

He had thought her reaction to him proved the truth of Peter's hysterical accusations. He hadn't said a word—he had avoided her, in fact—but she had known what he was thinking on the few occasions when they did meet, and it had sickened her. There had been a strange, bitter irony in his assumptions about her.

They stopped at a motorway café to have coffee at eleven. Kelly wandered off to inspect the pinball machines in the amusement area; she had had a Coke and some biscuits that she had rapidly demolished. Caroline stared at the plastic-topped table. The coffee was too hot to drink.

She felt Nick watching her. The sunlight gleamed on her soft loose curls. The wind had blown them into a tangle. No doubt she looked a mess, and she wished he would stop giving her that deadly stare. It made her blood run cold.

"Isn't it a beautiful day?" she said brightly, running a hand over her hair in the hope of smoothing it down.

"Isn't it?" His voice was derisive, and his blue eyes followed the nervous shift of her hand in a way that made her more nervous than ever.

"Does Helen know we're coming?"

"I rang her last night." He picked up his cup and drank some coffee, adding, "She cried."

Caroline bit her lower lip. "Oh, poor Helen."

"Yes, poor Helen," he drawled, eyeing her with sardonic speculation. "She's very attached to you." *Heaven knows why,* his blue eyes said, and Caroline felt her face heating again.

"I'm very fond of her," she stammered, and met his stare with defiance.

"Are you?" He made no attempt to hide his disbelief.

"Yes!"

"So fond that you haven't so much as sent her a Christmas card for three years," he murmured, one eyebrow lifted.

They were getting into difficult waters with that remark, and Caroline looked away across the crowded café. She saw Kelly in the distance, standing beside one of the pinball games and watching someone notch up a score in electric flashes.

"What exactly do you do at this advertising agency?" Nick asked, and Caroline turned back to him with a start.

"I'm a copywriter." Their eyes met and she said impatiently, "But of course you already know that. Your private detective would have investigated my job."

Nick shrugged those wide shoulders, his mouth amused. "I think he even found out what soap powder you use. He was a very thorough man."

"I don't think that's funny," Caroline snapped. "You had no right to send him snooping around me. It makes me feel sick to imagine him prying into my private life."

"Your private life kept its secrets," Nick said, his eyes hard. "He didn't come up with a shred of information about that."

"Make up your mind—you just said he even found out what soap powder I use!"

"But he didn't find out who you were sleeping with," Nick drawled, and with sardonic enjoyment watched the pink flood of color wash up her face.

"How disappointing for you," Caroline muttered, disliking him intensely.

"Unless, of course, you and this boss of yours have a discreet arrangement," Nick suggested. "My detective said he wasn't bad-looking."

"Oh, don't be absurd," she said, and he grinned.

"That will be a relief for Frey Forrester."

Caroline stiffened. She could not let him believe Peter's lies about Frey. Frey was a nice man, and it could be disastrous for a doctor to have gossip like that circulating about him. Frey's reputation had to be protected.

"There was never anything between Frey and me. Peter imagined things. I wasn't having an affair with anyone. There wasn't any other man."

He laughed under his breath but without amusement, eyeing her bitterly.

"It's true," she said, willing him to believe her. "I never looked at anyone else."

"Didn't you, Caroline?" There was fierce derision in his voice, and their eyes met, his blue stare burning into her, reminding her of a moment that even now had the ability to make her wince. Color rushed up into her face. She hurriedly looked away, pulses beating at her neck and temples.

She had been in the garden cutting roses when Nick walked down to bring her a message from Helen that tea was ready. It had been a late-autumn twilight, moths whispering around under the trees. Caroline had been nervous as she and Nick walked back to the house, and when a moth brushed her face she had given a muffled scream. Startled, Nick had bent over her, asking, "What's wrong?" She had looked up, eyes wide, half laughing as she realized her own stupidity in making such a fuss over a moth, and Nick had suddenly kissed her. She hadn't even hesitated. She had moved closer, an arm going around his neck, and kissed him back with a heady sense of crazy happiness that had no past and no future. Then Nick had broken off that deep hungry kiss and pushed past her to enter the house without a word, leaving her stunned and angry with herself.

It had never happened again. Nick had withdrawn entirely, his manner remote and unfriendly when they met, but no doubt the incident had left him with the distinct impression that Peter's suspicions about Caroline were not unfounded. If she was ready to kiss him like that, he must have decided, she would be equally approachable to someone else. Caroline had sometimes wondered if he had kissed her deliberately, to see how she would react, and she hated herself for the way she had responded. She had been giving evidence against herself without knowing what she was doing, and of course the last thing she would ever do was say to Nick, "The only man I ever looked at after I was married was you." Was he likely to believe her? And even if he did, how embarrassing, how humiliating, to confess as much!

Kelly came running back, and they left in silence.

Kelly was too busy talking to notice that. She was very excited about the journey and her enthusiasm spilled out as they drove on toward the north.

The flat fertile fields of the Midlands gave way to a more rugged landscape, the horizon hazy with rolling hills and rocky, heather-enriched moorland over which sheep grazed. Autumn was altering the color of the land from a rain-soaked green into the bronze and russet tints of drying bracken and withering heather, but purple bells still blew across the hills where the heather lasted longest.

Kelly was growing bored now. She said less and curled up with her brown head on the smooth upholstery, yawning. Caroline stared out of the car at the low stone walls meandering up hill, down dale, turning the landscape into a checkerboard.

She was far too aware of Nick's lean body beside her, his profile grim, his silence brooding. She forced herself to notice the flapping flight of a crow as it landed in a field they were passing; to absorb the destroyed abbey ruins on a hill above them, their stones mere jagged teeth thrust up from the grass; to take in the little villages they drove through, with their sturdy gray houses and slate roofs.

None of it made much sense to her in her present mood, but she pretended to be enthralled by it all because it meant she did not have to notice that grim silence.

The blue sky darkened slowly, and spots of rain began hitting the car windshield.

''It's raining,'' Kelly said, as though they might not have noticed, and Caroline brightly agreed that it was.

The windshield wipers began to click busily. The rain

thickened and the sky was gray and stormy, matching both the landscape and the atmosphere inside the car.

This was how she remembered Skeldale, she thought. It seemed the perfect weather for her to arrive in, the wind howling through the dales, the trees lashing frantically, leaves blowing in great drifts across the fields, their autumn tints darkening as rain soaked into them.

"Welcome home," Nick said with dry mockery, and she looked sideways and saw, amazingly, that he was smiling. It wasn't much of a smile, but it was one nonetheless.

As though he was happy to be home, he accelerated and the black car shot forward like a bullet from a gun, eating up the road so fast that the tires whined on the wet tarmac.

Skeldale was sheltered in a fold of the hills, moorland rising on either side of it, giving it cover from the howling winter gales. Helen lived on the far side of town, but to Caroline's surprise Nick did not take the narrow road down through the little town, but turned up a road to the left.

"Why are you going this way?" she asked, suddenly remembering that this road led to his own house.

"Helen's staying with me," he said expressionlessly.

She sat upright, stiffening.

"When she came out of hospital she wasn't in any state to look after herself. I invited her to move in with me until she had quite recovered."

Nervously Caroline said, "Oh, I see. That was kind of you." Her mind was racing; she was horrified at the idea that he might be expecting her to stay at his house, too. "We'll be able to get a room at that hotel in the

Market Square, won't we?'' she asked in a bright casual voice, hoping she sounded normal.

He gave her a sardonic look. "You'll stay at my house.''

"Oh, that's very kind, but—''

"But nothing,'' he said shortly.

"Really—'' she began, and he cut her off again.

"Your rooms are ready.''

Caroline would have gone on protesting if he hadn't silenced her with a grim, forbidding stare. She subsided in her seat, flushing. Well, it was only for a few days. She would just have to put up with it.

"It's good of you to take the trouble,'' she said nervously, and got another cold look.

"I haven't taken any trouble. My housekeeper looked after all that.''

"Do you still have Mrs. Bentall?'' Caroline vaguely remembered her, a thin spare woman with gray hair and a face that looked as if it had been carved out of the local granite.

"Yes.''

The car curved around a high-banked corner and the gray walls of the house showed through a scattering of trees. The sky was stormy behind it and a livid light flashed far off on the horizon where the storm was centered.

Caroline looked over her shoulder. Kelly was asleep, her head pillowed, her pink mouth slightly open, a flush on her cheeks. It would be a pity to wake her up. The journey had been tiring for her; she wasn't used to traveling long distances across country in a car.

Nick spun the wheel and the car slowed to drive

through high, open iron gates. Caroline looked at the square stone house curiously. She had been here only a few times and remembered it very vaguely. It looked smaller than she'd remembered, and the plain sensible architecture was diminished by the rolling grandeur of the moors behind it.

The car stopped outside the front door. Nick got out and walked around to open Caroline's door. She slid out beside him and then they both looked at Kelly. The child was still fast asleep, her regular breathing audible now that the engine had cut out.

"Now, Mrs. Storr...."

The dry impatient voice behind them made them both turn. Helen stood in the doorway with Mrs. Bentall behind her, trying to stop her from going out into the rain.

"You wait here and they'll come to you," Mrs. Bentall said in the indulgent scolding tone of a nanny to a child.

Caroline ran with her hands out, and Helen, tears in her eyes, whispered, "Oh, my dear, I didn't think I'd ever see you again!" Then, on an urgent note, "Where's Kelly? Didn't you bring her?"

Kissing her and hugging her, Caroline said, "She's in the car, fast asleep; it was too much for her."

Helen cried weakly, shivering in the wind from the moors. "I can't wait to see her! Oh, she'll have changed, and I missed it all, but you're here now, both of you, thank God."

"Come in out of that wind," Mrs. Bentall said. "Do you want to get pneumonia again, you silly woman?"

Laughing and crying, Helen said, "Nick, carry Kelly in. Bring her in, Nick."

"He'll bring her," Caroline said, pulling the older woman by the hand. "Come indoors, Helen; it's freezing out there."

There was a huge fire leaping up the great stone chimney, and the deep-upholstered chairs, the dark red carpet and velvet curtains made the room seem welcoming and homely.

"Sit down, Helen," Caroline said, but Helen wouldn't sit down. She was staring at the door, on tenterhooks, her pale face showing tiny patches of red in the middle of those gaunt cheeks. She had never been anything but thin. Now she was hollow faced and frail; you could see the delicate bones under her skin. Her hair was turning white and she looked old, far older than her sixty years.

Caroline's heart ached as she watched her, and then Nick came in carrying a sleepy Kelly, who looked about her, blinking in the light and the warmth of the fire, her little face very flushed and her eyes very bright.

"Kelly, love," Helen said.

Nick looked sharply at her. "Sit down," he barked, his face impatient, and Helen sat, like an obedient child, but held out her arms as Kelly ran and climbed onto her lap.

CHAPTER THREE

THAT EVENING when Kelly had been tucked into bed, Nick discreetly vanished, saying he had to call on a friend, and Caroline and Helen sat talking by the roaring fire. Helen's face had a great deal more color as she gazed at the flames leaping up the chimney. She had spent the whole afternoon with her granddaughter, and Caroline had watched them with faint anxiety: there was something heart-wrenching in the way Helen couldn't take her eyes off the little girl's face. Caroline was afraid she was too keyed up. She looked so frail—too much excitement might not be good for her. So Caroline had kept a close watch, ready at any moment to persuade Helen to go and rest if she showed signs of exhaustion.

Glancing at the clock now, she said with a smile, "You really ought to bed in bed, Helen."

"Nonsense." Helen bridled, giving her a cheerful grimace. "Don't you start fussing. Mrs. Bentall is bad enough."

"She's right; it has been a tiring day for you."

"I feel better than I have for weeks," Helen said. "Oh, my dear, I have missed you, both of you. I can't tell you how glad I am to have you back."

"We're glad to be back; we both missed you."

Caroline hesitated. "Helen, I hated leaving like that, knowing how you would worry about us, but—"

"I know." Helen broke in, her smile going. "I understood."

"I didn't dare let you know where we were." No sooner had she said that than she wished she hadn't. Helen had understood. Saying it aloud didn't make it any easier to bear. Caroline bit her lip, looking at the older woman anxiously.

"I'm sorry."

"You're the last person in the world to need to say, 'I'm sorry,'" Helen told her with flat determination. "It's I who should be saying it to you. You put up with the situation for as long as you could."

"I'd have gone on putting up with it if it hadn't been for Kelly."

"Yes," Helen said, her eyes going to the fire.

There was a silence for a few moments. The wind howled in the chimney, rain spat down among the logs and little green flames shot out from the crackling wood.

"Kelly seems so different," Helen said abruptly. "You've done a good job. I was afraid she would be scarred for life."

"So was I." Caroline thought of the painting on her wall at home. The black shadow had been withdrawn from her daughter's life. Kelly wouldn't entirely forget it; that was too much to ask. But she was able to push it to the far recesses of her memory now, walling it in with happier memories. The past three years had given Kelly the normal, secure environment all children have the right to expect and which must be the base on which the rest of their lives can rest.

"I wasn't sure what I would see," Helen said, disturbing her. "Three years is a long time."

"Was it very long, Helen?" Caroline looked at her with compassion. Helen had been disturbed, worried, nervous before Caroline left Skeldale, but now she was a ghost of the woman she had been when Caroline first met her.

Their eyes met. "It wasn't easy," confessed Helen. "He became more and more violent, and the drinking came out in the open. Frey tried to persuade him to go into hospital, but that only made things worse. He hated Frey too much to listen, and Frey couldn't force him. Peter wouldn't see another doctor, refused to admit he was an alcoholic, said he could stop whenever he wanted to, but why should he? It was the only thing that kept him sane, he said. He wasn't giving up his only chance of a few hours' pleasure."

Caroline had known what sort of pattern had been woven into the years since she left Skeldale. It had been laid down long before. At first neither she nor Helen had realized how serious Peter's problem was. He was cunning enough to hide it for a while, and when they did understand that he had become dependent on drink, they found themselves cooperating with him to hide it. Helen couldn't face the thought of anyone finding out. She was so horrified she wept like a child, begged Caroline not to tell anyone. Peter was shaken by their realization. He had promised to stop drinking and for a few weeks had kept his promise, then some incident at work started him off again. Caroline had tried to reason with him, and that was when the violence had begun.

In drunken rage he had beaten her up so badly that

Helen sent for Frey, who did not believe their story that Caroline had fallen downstairs, and again Peter had sworn he would turn over a new leaf, never touch a drink, if only they would forgive him. He was genuinely contrite. He had cried and kissed Caroline pleadingly, looking at her bruised face with horror at himself.

Frey had patiently worn Caroline down over the next few months until he was able to persuade her to admit the truth.

"He must have treatment," he had said. "He's sick, Caroline. He needs professional help."

"He's trying to stop," she told him. "He really tries, Frey. Helen and I search the house every morning. He hides the liquor."

"Yes," Frey had said, looking at her dryly. "I know. I've heard the same story too many times. It's a problem that's on the increase, even in little towns like Skeldale. My dear girl, you and his mother can't help him. Only Peter can help himself, but he needs advice and support from people who understand the problem. I'll give you a number to ring if ever you want to get help. These people will come at any time of the night and day. They've been through it themselves and they know all about it."

They had tried, but everything had failed because Frey just could not persuade Peter to admit what was wrong. Peter found reasons to explain his drinking: his work was going badly; he was depressed; he had been at a party and the drinks had been forced on him. Every time he thought up a new excuse.

It wasn't long before he had found one that was the

perfect cover. He disliked seeing Frey because Frey knew the truth. Frey's clear gray eyes saw too much, and Peter was made uneasy by meeting them. He knew Caroline confided in Frey by then, and he resented it. He began resenting it aloud, in public, but because he did not want anyone to know the true reason for his hatred of Frey, he claimed to believe that Caroline and Frey were seeing too much of each other. He was careful not to imply that they were lovers, because he was afraid Frey might challenge him and even threaten libel action. Peter did not want any public confrontation that might reveal the truth about his drinking.

From suspicion of Frey it had been an easy step to the realization that people were sympathetic to his jealousy over Caroline, and that jealousy gave him the all-purpose excuse he needed.

Caroline had to put up with jealous scenes if she even spoke to a man. She shrank into herself and rarely went out. She avoided Frey as she avoided everyone else. The house had become a place of shadows, unexpressed fears, nervous apprehension. It had been the final straw when Peter began hitting Kelly. He did it only when he was half-crazy with drink. Helen and Caroline tried to keep the little girl out of his way, but that wasn't always possible. Caroline had been afraid; she had been terrified, night and day, of what might happen to Kelly.

So in the end she had run. Her father had emigrated to Australia just before her marriage in order to live near his sister in Sydney, and when he died, leaving Caroline quite a large sum of money, she decided to vanish with Kelly before something terrible happened.

She had not stopped loving Peter all at once. The love had seeped away gradually until her heart was empty and all she felt for him was fear and pain. When you have lived with tensions like that for some time it is hard to wind down and learn to face outward again, meet life openly and without fear.

"I wish you hadn't had to face it on your own," she told Helen, her face flushed by the firelight. "I wish I'd been here when he was killed." They had learned to talk to each other without saying too much. Words were rarely adequate, anyway. Helen and Caroline had lived in a tacit conspiracy of silence for so long that they could fill in the gaps between the words, reach each other without saying aloud what their eyes revealed.

"The worst part," Helen began, and stopped.

"I know," Caroline said huskily. She knew the worst, the terrible relief and release. They had both been through it.

"I can't help feeling there might have been something I could have done."

"There wasn't," Caroline said in a firm voice. "We tried everything."

"There must have been something." It was the helpless inability to reach him that was so bitter. Helen's thin fingers writhed on her lap. "I was his mother; I should have been able to help him."

"Frey said the only one who could help him was himself," Caroline reminded her.

"We were too strict with him when he was a baby, when he was growing up," Helen said, staring at the flickering flames. "His father was a stern man, old-fashioned, I suppose. He had clear-cut ideas about how a boy should be brought up. Peter was beaten too often—oh, not seriously, but he was very highly strung. He took it badly when his father caned him."

"I've never hit Kelly," Caroline said. "Never. I don't believe in it." Kelly had been terrified of violence. Even the small smack any other mother might give a child who was naughty had been out of the question for Kelly.

"Nor do I," Helen said flatly. "Not now. I wish I had understood better when Peter was small, but in those days it was normal; it seemed normal to me. Teachers caned children in schools in those days."

"Don't blame yourself," Caroline said, going over to kneel beside her and take her hands. "You mustn't brood over it, Helen. I don't think it was being caned as a boy that warped Peter. He was just weak."

It had shown in other ways, the flaw that had widened over the years until what had once been a barely visible hairline crack had become a gulf in the center of his nature. A man does not destroy himself and those around him unless he is seriously inadequate.

Helen gripped her fiercely. "Oh, I'm glad you're home. The only person I could talk to was Frey, and he's so busy, I couldn't take up much of his time. I needed so badly to talk to someone. I kept going over and over it in my own mind until I thought I'd go mad."

"Talk as much as you like," Caroline said. She would rather not hear any more of it, but if talking would ease Helen's brooding misery she would listen till the cows came home. For the past three years she had devoted all her own energies to forgetting Peter, burying him in the past, to ease her own mind and to wipe out those black shadows from Kelly's life. Helen had had to live with the problem all that time, and Caroline felt guilty about it. She had left Helen to cope with a situation she herself had found intolerable, and it was no use telling herself that she had fled for Kelly's sake, because although that was true, a little cold voice kept asking her how much of her concern had been for Kelly and how much for herself. She had no answer to that acute question; she just did not know.

In the firelight Helen talked in a low flat voice, and Caroline listened, getting a bitter picture of all Helen had been through. The grandfather clock in the hall chimed sonorously and they both started.

"Ten o'clock! You really should be in bed."

Helen yawned, looking surprised. "Do you know, you're right. I'm tired. I've almost talked myself to sleep."

Caroline laughed. "I'll come up with you. I'm tired, too. It was such a long drive, although Nick's car goes at a fantastic speed. I was scared out of my wits on the motorway."

"Didn't Kelly love it, though? Didn't she just? Never stopped talking about it. She wasn't scared, was she? Quite fearless." Helen stopped short, looking at Caroline with wide startled eyes. Slowly she said it again: "Quite fearless, thank God."

Caroline put an arm around her and led her out of the room without answering. Helen was painfully thin, her dress hanging loosely on her, and it seemed to Caroline that she hardly weighed as much as Kelly.

The wind wailed under the heavy oak front door as they walked through the hall, and the carpet flapped eerily beside them. If she had been in her own little bungalow she would have been scared to death by noises like that. When you live alone you are prey to fears that vanish in the cold clear light of day.

She said good-night to Helen and went into her own room. When she was ready for bed she went to check that Kelly was safely asleep. Kelly always slept curled up, one arm flung over her head, and every night Caroline kissed her softly and tucked that arm back under the bedclothes.

She crept out again a moment later, but as she closed Kelly's door a movement behind her made her swing around in shock, a hand flying to her mouth in a childish gesture of alarm as she saw the dark figure looming there in the hall.

Nick stared at her with narrowed eyes, and she let out her held breath, flushing.

"I didn't hear you," she muttered, annoyed with herself.

His stare moved assessingly over her and she quivered under that insolent probe, feeling his eyes like a burning brand on the creamy sweep of her throat, smooth breasts and half-glimpsed shoulders. The white lace of her negligee was more decorative than concealing. Her skin glimmered through it, and Nick's lazy inspection roamed all the way down to her feet while Caroline seethed impotently.

"Waiting for *me*, Caroline?" he drawled, his mouth curling.

She tried to dive past him and he sidestepped into

her path. Caroline looked up to make an angry protest, but the brooding intentness of his eyes held her
silent, her face burning. She became deeply aware of
the stormy night outside the house, the silence inside,
their isolation together, and her heart began thudding
against her breastbone.

"Have you been waiting long?" he said in that low
taunting voice, and she heard the ambiguity and mockery in the words perfectly clearly.

The shiver she gave made his mouth twist in a smile
of cruel satisfaction. "Cold?" he asked, moving so
close that their bodies almost touched. He put a long
finger on her bare shoulder where the neckline of her
nightdress plunged, and her breath caught in the back
of her throat. The finger began to descend, trailing between her breasts.

"Don't," she muttered angrily, pushing his hand
away, and he laughed under his breath.

Trembling, bitterly angry, she met his eyes, hating
him. Her skin was prickling with sensual reaction
where he had touched it, and from the expression in
the blue eyes, Nick knew that.

She slid past in an agitated movement and this time
he let her go. Caroline closed her door and stumbled
over to her bed. She hated herself almost as much as
she hated him.

The bedroom was dark. There was no moon and
there were no streetlights out here on the edge of the
moors. Her own feelings obsessed her as she pulled
back the covers and fell into bed, a hurt so deep that it
seemed to suffocate her. She turned over and buried
her face in the pillow to shut out the pain.

WHEN SHE CAME DOWN the next morning the sky was a deep vivid blue. Nick was eating a piece of toast, a newspaper in one hand. He looked up, his blue eyes shooting over her in a rapid narrowed glance that made her feel stupidly breathless.

"Good morning," she said brightly. "A wonderful morning, isn't it?"

"Wonderful," he said, the sardonic expression not lost on her. He was far too aware of the effect he had on her, and she swung away to sit down, her lashes drooping against her flushed cheeks.

"What are you and Helen planning to do today?" he inquired, wiping his fingers on his napkin.

"Just take things as they come," Caroline said, pouring herself some coffee. "She said she usually stays in bed until quite late."

He nodded. "She has to rest a good deal."

"Of course." Caroline reached over to take a slice of toast and Nick watched her, making her so nervous that she dropped it before it reached her plate.

"I'll get Mrs. Bentall to make some more," he said dryly.

"No, don't bother...."

"It's no bother," he informed her, the derisive bite in his voice making her shrink. "That's what she is paid for."

"I'm really not hungry."

He ignored that, ringing the bell, and Mrs. Bentall bustled into the room, a large white apron tied around her waist.

"More toast? Would you like something cooked first, Mrs. Storr? Eggs and bacon?"

"No, thank you," Caroline said, smiling back at her. "But Kelly likes to have a boiled egg for breakfast. She's still asleep, and I decided to leave her for a while."

"Oh, aye," Mrs. Bentall agreed approvingly. "Let the little lass sleep."

When she had gone Caroline sipped her coffee, staring out of the window. The moors were flooded with sunlight that turned the remaining leaves on the trees a glittering bronze. There seemed to be no wind. Along the distant horizon a soft blue haze lingered like smoke from an autumn fire. She stared at it fixedly, conscious of the insistent probe of Nick's eyes like icy needles under her skin. He wanted her to be aware of that cold stare, and although it annoyed her, she was unable to ignore it.

He got up and she jumped, her eyes flying to him nervously as he walked around the table toward her. He paused and gave her a mocking little smile. "I'm off to work. Enjoy yourself."

She heard the door click shut and closed her eyes. It was going to be very hard to live in the same house as a man who treated her like that.

The morning passed quietly. Over lunch Kelly kept asking if they could take Nick's two dogs for a walk, and Caroline promised that they would go later.

"Frey should drop in this afternoon," Helen said. "I owe that man so much!"

Kelly looked up, shocked. "Do you owe him a lot of money?"

"No, dear, not money," Helen said, smiling.

Kelly looked faintly disappointed. "What, then?"

she asked, and got a shake of the head. She went back to counting plum pits, murmuring, "Tinker, tailor... I'm going to marry a poor man, I'm going to marry a poor man...."

"Are we going for this walk right away or shall we go later?" Caroline asked hopefully, but Kelly said they would go right away.

She couldn't wait to be out in the sunlight with the great golden dogs. Kelly had no pet, for Caroline felt it would be unkind to have any sort of animal in the bungalow when they were both out all day. Kelly had argued that Deirdre wouldn't mind looking after it, and Deirdre and Caroline had made faces at each other in amusement. "Oh, wouldn't I just?" Deirdre had demanded. "You've got a nerve, Miss Kelly Storr."

It had been one of the rare occasions when Caroline had denied her daughter something she really wanted, and she had been relieved when Kelly had accepted the decision with good grace. Her instinct was always to give Kelly what she wanted, if she could, because she felt she had so much to make up to the little girl.

Helen went upstairs to rest and the dogs tore off onto the moors with Caroline and Kelly following them. The sun was no longer so warm and a wind had sprung up, whistling through the springy heather and making the clouds scud across the sky above them. Caroline wandered along, breathing in the fresh clean scents of the moorland, watching the rapidly changing sky, feeling free and unafraid in the last of the autumn sunlight. Kelly was laughing as she ran with the dogs, their tails swishing with excitement.

They walked farther than she had intended, and

Kelly was dragging her feet as they got back to the house. "I'm tired, mummy, I'm tired. Can't you carry me?"

"Carry a big girl like you? Mummy certainly won't." Neither of them had heard anyone behind them as they came down the heather-rough slope toward the garden wall, and Kelly jumped in surprise, looking around.

Caroline stopped. She recognized that voice. Swinging around, she held out a hand, her face lighting up.

"Frey!"

He held her hand in both of his, smiling: a large, calm, fair man whose sleek hair was beginning to show some streaks of gray but whose face had a quiet warmth that could be very comforting.

"How are you, Caroline?"

"I'm fine—how are you? You look very well." He looked almost exactly the same as he had the last time she saw him. Perhaps there were a few more gray streaks, perhaps his face had gathered a few lines, but his smile was precisely the same and she was delighted to see him.

"Busy," he said, still holding her hand. "Yes, you look much better than you did the last time we met." The gray eyes were shrewdly scrutinizing her: not much missed Frey. He didn't say much, either, but people instinctively trusted him and he was adored by most of his patients, particularly the female ones. He was never too busy to listen or to notice if something was wrong.

Kelly waited, her face curious, and he looked down at her and released her mother to say, "Well, well, well, and is this Kelly? What has your mummy been feeding you on?"

Kelly grinned, recognizing that this was an adult joke, and Frey said, "I wouldn't have known you; do you remember me?"

"No," Kelly said honestly.

"And why should you?" Frey teased her. "I'm Dr. Forrester."

"Why does mummy call you Frey, then?"

He gave Caroline an amused look. "Because your mummy knows me very well and Frey is my first name."

"I never heard that name before—it's a funny name." Kelly too often said exactly what was in her mind.

"My mother was Norwegian," he told her. "Frey comes from an old Norse name."

"What's Norse?"

"She never stops asking questions if you let her start," Caroline told him, laughing apologetically.

"And a good thing, too," he said. "How's she to find out anything if she doesn't ask questions?"

Kelly looked pleased: this was a man she liked. Frey took her hand and helped her over the wall into the garden, explaining to her about Norse legends as he walked beside her up the narrow winding path toward the house. The garden was littered with rain-soaked leaves and fallen branches from last night's storm. Clumps of Michaelmas daisies, a few pink asters and some chrysanthemums gave a little color to the flower beds, but the cold finger of winter lay on the rest of the garden and the trees were almost bare except for a few that were choked with dark climbing ivy.

The house was warm and inviting when they walked into it through the garden door. "I've come to see

Helen,'' Frey told Caroline. "How do you think she looks?"

Caroline glanced at Kelly and then at him. "I wish she looked better," she said discreetly.

Frey glanced at Kelly, too. "I wonder where your grandma is," he said, and Kelly at once offered to go look for her.

When she had gone, Frey moved to the fireplace and leaned there, his face thoughtful. "She only just made it back to us," he told Caroline. "It was touch and go. I thought I'd lost her at one time—I wish I could say I pulled her through, but it was Nick who did the magic trick."

"Nick?" Caroline's voice was sharp.

"He promised her he would find you and Kelly. Peter had tried in the past and given up looking, but Nick swore he'd find you if he had to scour the whole country himself." Frey smiled at her. "And of course, being Nick, he kept his promise, and here you are."

Caroline moved over and put another log on the fire. "Helen will pick up strength now, won't she? She looks like a walking corpse."

"Her heart isn't strong and she's no longer young, but with the right incentive she should live for years."

"The right incentive?" Caroline echoed, smiling.

"Kelly," Frey told her.

"Kelly and I can't stay here," Caroline said slowly. "I've got a very good job in London."

"So I gather. Copywriter with some advertising agency, Nick said."

She nodded. "It pays very well and I enjoy the work. We've got a bungalow and Kelly is doing well at school. I wouldn't want to uproot her now." She hesitated. "The problem is, my bungalow has only two bedrooms. I suppose Kelly could share my room and Helen could have the other one. It would work for a year or two."

Frey considered the idea, pushing back his fair hair. "Wait a few days, Caroline; give yourself time to think before you rush into suggesting that. For the moment all that matters to Helen is that she's got you both back."

Caroline's eyes filled stupidly with tears and Frey exclaimed under his breath, moving closer to her. "My dear girl, I'm sorry! What did I say? Clumsy of me."

She laughed, eyes wet, then gave a silly hiccup, and Frey put a hand on her windswept blond curls and drew her close to him until her head rested on his shoulder. She hid her face, shaking and crossly asking herself why she was making a fool of herself now when she had been perfectly fine all day. Frey must think her an idiot, bursting into tears without reason.

A sound made them draw apart. Caroline looked around before she had stopped to think—and tensed as she saw Nick in the doorway, regarding them coldly, his blue eyes narrowed to metallic slits.

"Sorry to interrupt," he bit out.

Frey had a faint flush. "Hello, Nick," he said in an overly cheerful tone.

"I wondered when we would see *you* here," Nick said with sardonic stress.

Frey's pale brows lifted. "I call on Helen most days," he answered dryly.

Caroline had turned away to brush a hand over her

wet eyes. How dared Nick speak to Frey like that! Her face was flushed, her body stiff with outrage.

Helen came in with Kelly, and Caroline excused herself to go upstairs to wash and change. She put on a warm sweater and black pleated skirt and sat in front of the dressing table brushing her ruffled hair, her eyes angry.

There was a tap on her door. She called, "Come in," expecting to see Mrs. Bentall or Helen, but it was Nick in his dark business suit, his tie loose, his jacket open, looking withdrawn and cool as their eyes met in the mirror.

"I've asked Forrester to dinner. I'm sure you'll approve."

She answered in a voice as chilly, "It's your house."

"I thought you might like warning." He ran his glance over her reflection dismissively. "I'm sure you can do better than a skirt and sweater—for him."

She was tempted to pick up something from the dressing table and chuck it at him. Who on earth did he think he was, talking to her like that?

He read the spark of rebellion in the green eyes and looked at her mockingly. "Just remember, you're under my roof and I'm not standing by and watching you playing games with Forrester, so keep him at a distance."

"You have no right—" she began, lifting her chin defiantly, her fingers curling around the brush she held as though she were about to throw it.

He broke into her words, his mouth twisting. "You'll find I assume any right I choose to," he drawled.

"Not with me," Caroline flared.

He leaned against the door, his long body casually elegant, but under the smooth material of the suit was a controlled physical power that was a silent threat.

"Helen wanted me to invite Forrester," he said. "I had no choice at the time. But don't imagine for one second that he is here for you or that I'm going to let you start up your affair with him again."

Her face burned. "I've told you—"

"And I don't believe you." The blue eyes had an electrically charged rage in them that made Caroline feel weak and helpless. "I shall be watching you all evening," he said. "Remember that."

To cover her disturbed state she began to brush her hair again, her fingers not quite steady. She expected him to leave the room, but he stayed where he was, watching her intently in the mirror, and a slow prickle of awareness passed down her spine at the look in the blue eyes.

Her face began to burn and her eyes moved hurriedly away, her lashes flickering very fast as she tried to hide her reaction. Nick laughed under his breath, as though she had satisfied him by her unnerved response, and then he went out, closing the door behind him with a snap.

Caroline shut her eyes, swallowing. That look had been another of his calculated sexual insults, and it had certainly achieved what he had set out to do— made her feel miserable.

She would never be able to convince him that he was wrong about her. He would always see her in a distorted light. Even if she produced Helen and Frey to back up her story, what would Nick think but that they were either lying or ignorant of the truth?

He knew Helen's fondness for her, and he would believe that Helen had no idea what she was really like. And as for poor Frey, how could he ever hope to be believed? Nick would suspect every word the doctor said, for if Frey had been her lover while she was his patient, he was never going to admit it because it could ruin his professional life.

She was trapped in a bitter situation from which there was no easy way out, and while Nick had the chance he was going to needle and mock and hurt her as much as he could.

CHAPTER FOUR

SHE TURNED TOWARD THE DOOR a few moments later, intending to go down as she was, in the skirt and sweater. Then a sudden gust of defiance hit her. *Why the hell should I,* she thought, swinging around. She marched over to the wardrobe and got down a simple blue shift, its classic style coolly sophisticated. Zipping up the dress a moment later, she caught a glimpse of herself in the mirror, her face very flushed, her eyes dangerously bright. Anger was racing in her veins.

She hunted for a bottle of perfume, touched all her pulse points with the light fragrance and took more trouble over her face and hair. It was a long time since she had deliberately paid so much attention to her appearance. You got out of the habit when your mind was concerned mainly with getting from A to B in a tearing hurry, and the last thing she had wanted to do was make any of the men in the agency sit up and notice her. Men had been on her list of things she could do without.

When she got downstairs, Frey was talking to Helen by the fire. They both looked around. Helen smiled in surprise and delight, and Frey whistled softly under his breath, grinning.

"Hello, hello, hello," he said as she swayed across

the room toward them on her very high white shoes.

"Frey's having dinner with us," Helen said.

"Touch wood," he agreed. "Unless I get called out."

"How nice." Caroline sat down smoothly, crossing her legs, and looked at Helen. "Kelly wasn't in her room. Where has she got to?"

"She's helping Mrs. Bentall. You don't mind, do you? Kelly begged to be allowed to help."

"I don't mind at all. She loves being in the kitchen."

Frey was nursing a glass of sherry, and he asked, "Can I get you something to drink?"

"Sherry would be lovely," she said, smiling at him. Helen got up with the careful movements of someone who is not quite sure she will make it, and Caroline started to get up, too.

"Stay there," Helen said lightly. "I can manage. Every day I get better."

Caroline's smile hurt. "Of course you do."

Helen slowly crossed the room. Frey was pouring sherry, but his oblique glance followed her progress and a frown etched itself between his brows.

When the door had closed behind her, Caroline said in a low voice, "I hate watching her."

"She's going to be all right," Frey promised, coming back to hand her the glass of sherry. "It just takes time. Rome wasn't built in a day."

"You should come and work for us," Caroline teased. "My boss would love your clichés."

"What impudence," he said, pinching her chin. "How did you get this job?"

"By sheer fluke. I was working there as a secretary, my boss was taken ill, and I came up with one or two ideas to finish the project she had been working on. So they asked if I'd like to have a crack at doing that sort of thing, and of course I jumped at it. Within six months I was doing it full-time."

"I'm impressed," Frey said.

"It's just a knack."

"A useful knack to have."

Caroline smiled. "Oh, the money's much better, but there's far more strain. When you're just a secretary you work nine to five-thirty, and if there's a problem it isn't your baby, but I'm responsible for whatever I'm working on and I often have to take work home and give up a whole weekend to it."

Frey regarded her wryly. "That's not so good. You mustn't work too hard. You can't keep it up forever, especially when you have Kelly to think about. It won't do her any good if you crack up."

"I wouldn't let it come to that." Caroline shrugged. "I'm not that ambitious. Copywriting pays well, but it is just a job and Kelly means far more to me."

Frey had sat down in the chair beside her. He finished his sherry and put the glass down, leaning back with a sigh. "This is very pleasant. I can't believe I'm going to get through a whole evening without being summoned away."

She looked at him teasingly through her lashes. "Aren't you the guy who just warned me not to work too hard?"

He grimaced. "I haven't much choice. My partner isn't a young man anymore."

Nick strolled into the room and stood there, his long body at ease, his blue eyes watchful. "Can I get you another drink, Forrester?" The offer was made very coolly.

"No, thank you. I have to limit myself to one sherry in case I get called out later."

Nick shrugged and went over to the decanter. He came back with his glass in his hand and leaned near the fireplace, eyeing them.

"The conversation seems to have dried up," he murmured dryly when neither of them spoke.

"How's the factory?" Frey began.

"Is it still raining?" Caroline asked at the same time, and they both stopped and laughed in an embarrassed way. Nick's sardonic stare made them uneasy.

"The factory is ticking over nicely, and yes, it is still raining," Nick informed them with unhidden derision.

Caroline looked at him with irritation, and his bland mockery in return made her color rise.

"Doesn't Caroline look charming?" Frey asked, smiling at her, and Nick laughed shortly.

"That wasn't the word I was searching for."

What word had he been searching for? Caroline met his gaze and could guess that it had not been a flattering one.

Frey looked at her and then at Nick. "Is it a game? Are we expected to guess?"

Nick switched his blue stare to him, his hard mouth straight. "Guess away," he snarled, and Caroline's color burned hotly in her averted face.

Looking surprised, Frey said, "Word games aren't really my cup of tea."

"What sort of games do you prefer?" Nick drawled icily, his black brows jerking together.

His hostility was right out in the open and the whole atmosphere in the firelit room had changed. They had been sitting there talking quietly like old friends, but now Caroline felt an electric charge in the air and she bit her lip to stop herself from flying out at Nick with furious denials that he would only laugh at.

Frey had a curious, puzzled expression. He watched Nick with those clear gray eyes, searching his frowning face for some clue to his mood.

The telephone rang. Frey sighed. "A hundred to one that's for me."

Nick was already on his way to the door. "I'll get it."

Frey sank back, staring after him. "He's in a difficult mood," he said quietly to Caroline. "Is something wrong?"

Unhappily she said, "I'm sorry he snapped like that." What on earth must Frey be thinking?

"I suppose he's another one who works too hard," Frey said dryly. "It must be some sort of contagious disease." He glanced at the door again. "It looks as if it wasn't for me, after all. Maybe this is my lucky night."

Kelly darted into the room in pajamas and dressing gown. "I've come to kiss you good-night. I made jam tarts, but you're having apple pie for dinner. I cored the apples." She threw her arms around Caroline and kissed her, then gave Frey one of her cheerful grins. "And liver," she added.

"I like liver," Frey said. "Don't I get a good-night kiss?"

Kelly backed away, shaking her head.

"I'll come up with you," Caroline said. "Excuse me, Frey."

They went out, passing Nick as he put down the phone. Caroline felt his cold stare following her as she walked toward the stairs. It wasn't pleasant to be watched with that grim dislike. What right did he think he had to sit in judgment on her? What business was it of his if she sat talking to Frey in the firelight?

Kelly was talking quickly, excitedly, and with half her mind Caroline listened to her daughter while the other half angrily considered what she would like to do to Nick Holt. He was ruining her visit. How could she enjoy being with Helen again, seeing Skeldale and the moors, when every time she turned around she felt those icy blue eyes stripping her?

"Good night, darling," she said, kissing Kelly before she put out the light.

"Can't I have a story?"

Caroline certainly wasn't in a hurry to go down again. She sat on the bed in the darkness and told Kelly a story, but before she had reached the end of it Kelly was half-asleep, her head curled on her hand. Caroline crept out, closing the door quietly, but a little voice said, "Night, night, mummy," and she laughed as she went downstairs.

Helen was with the two men. It made things easier because Nick was cloaking his antagonism in Helen's presence, and over dinner conversation was quite friendly, although when Frey absentmindedly put up a hand to brush one of Caroline's loose blond curls away from her face, Nick's eyes narrowed sharply on them both and Caroline's stomach plunged at the expression that passed over his face.

It was as they were drinking their coffee that Mrs. Bentall came in softly and said, "Telephone, doctor."

"I knew it," Frey said, sighing as he got up.

"Oh, what a pity," Helen said.

Frey went out and came back in a moment, shrugging into his overcoat. "Mrs. Fraser," he told them, looking at Helen.

She sat up. "What's happened?" Mrs. Fraser was a friend of hers, a large florid woman in her fifties with three grown children. Helen's anxious eyes watched Frey as he answered.

"Her arthritis has flared up again. We've had some very wet weather lately, and she always has trouble in this sort of weather. I'll have to give her an injection."

"Oh dear," Helen said. "Poor Janet...give her my love. I do hope it isn't serious."

"Painful rather than serious," Frey said. He turned to look at Nick, his eyes a little guarded because he had picked up Nick's hostility and was not quite sure what was behind it. "I had a most enjoyable evening, thank you. You must all have dinner with me sometime soon."

Nick inclined his head coolly but didn't say anything, his strong mouth a hard line.

Frey paused, then turned to Caroline and smiled. "Good night—it's good to have you back with us. Be seeing you, I hope."

"I hope so," she said, smiling brightly, defiance in her eyes as she felt Nick watching her. Frey was her friend and she wasn't chopping off her friends just because Nick Holt ordered it.

When he had gone Helen said, "That is a very good man."

"Yes," Caroline agreed rather too vehemently, her eyes meeting the sideways look she got from Nick. He could glare as much as he liked!

Yawning, Helen stood up. "I think I'll go to bed; I'm really quite tired."

"So am I," Caroline said hurriedly. She had no intention of being left alone with Nick.

"Finish your coffee," Nick commanded her curtly, and Helen smiled.

"Yes, stay and finish your coffee, dear. You don't want to go to bed this early." She turned toward the door and Caroline rose, meaning to follow, but Nick's fingers bit around her wrist, holding her back. She tugged uselessly, not daring to say a word while Helen was in earshot, humiliated by her inability to break free and furious with Nick for his insistence.

Once Helen had closed the door without looking back, Caroline hissed at him, "Let go of me!"

"Sit down," he said, eyeing her flushed face with amusement.

"Let go!"

"Not until you do what you're told," he said softly.

For a few seconds their eyes warred in angry silence, then she gave in and sat. His fingers released her and she pointedly looked at the red mark on her wrist.

"Finish your coffee," Nick ordered.

Tight-lipped, she picked up the cup. He watched her lift it to her lips, her loose soft curls tumbling over her shoulder as she tilted back her head. His brows jerked together and the blue eyes took on a metallic glitter.

"And I don't want to see Forrester handling you again."

Her cup went down with a little crash as it hit the saucer. She looked at him in fury. "He did nothing of the kind!"

"No?" Nick's hand seized her blond hair and let it run through his fingers, watching the warm gleam of it as if it fascinated him. "He did that," he said. "A very intimate little gesture for a doctor to make to a patient, wasn't it?"

Caroline wanted to hit him. "You had no business talking to Frey the way you did. Your manner was downright insulting!"

His mouth hardened. "Maybe I'm a little sickened by hearing Helen talk about him as if he were a saint, when you and I know what went on between the two of you behind her back."

"Nothing went on!"

"Tell that to the marines," he muttered, a dark flare of color in his cheeks.

She counted to ten in her head. She had to talk to him patiently, make him see how insane his suspicions were.

"Can you really believe that a man like Frey Forrester would have done such a thing as to have an affair with a married patient? You must know how disastrous it would have been for him. It could have destroyed his career if it had got out. Frey has far too much common sense and decency to let himself get involved in anything like that."

Nick's mouth twisted fiercely, bitter mockery in his eyes. "I'm sure it weighed heavily on his conscience. I agree, Forrester's a decent guy, but he would have had to be a hair-shirted monk to resist the temptation you offered him, and I doubt if he's that." His eyes were fixed on her face, the narrowed glitter of them making her flinch.

"I didn't offer Frey anything," she whispered, her skin very cold. "Nick, please believe me—"

"Believe you?" he threw back in a barbed tone. "Honey, I'm not the sort of blind idiot you're apparently used to dealing with! I know exactly what you are and I'll never believe a single word you tell me unless I can check it out myself."

"Ask Frey," she stammered, incoherent with pain and resentment at the way he was talking to her.

"Ask *him*?" Nick laughed shortly. "What sort of fool do you take me for? Of course he would deny it. What else could he do?"

Caroline had known what he would say, of course. She might as well have saved her breath.

"I had to sit and listen to Peter eating his heart out over you," Nick muttered. "He drank to forget you and in the end he managed to kill himself—except, of course, that we both know who killed him, don't we?"

She shrank from the icy hostility in his face, shaking her head miserably. "It isn't true! I'm not like that."

He laughed unpleasantly. "Oh, you're not? Well, I couldn't believe it at first, I admit. I knew only what I saw of you then, and I was as taken in by the big green eyes and sweet smile as the rest of them. I doubted my own ears when Peter first told me. I thought he was crazy." He looked at her with stabbing ferocity. "Until you showed me that he wasn't imagining a thing. . . ."

A wave of hot color ran up her face and she looked down, her eyes distraught.

He leaned toward her, his voice harsh. "I was tempted. I'll admit that."

Caroline's eyes flicked up briefly, wide and shimmering with unshed tears, and Nick ran a glance over her with an unhidden but brutal desire that made her feel sick.

"You aren't denying *that*, I notice," he told her icily, and she stared at her hands without answering. How could she deny it? Even to stammer out a denial would be to betray herself, because she knew her voice would be unsteady and filled with disturbed emotion.

Nick waited, then said, "Well, go on, tell me I imagined that you invited me to make a pass at you."

She swallowed and somehow found the strength to say, "I can't deny you made a pass. I didn't invite it." That, at least, was partially true. She had not invited it, but when it came she had not rejected it. Having forced herself to speak, she managed to get up, too, saying as coolly as she could, "I certainly did not want it."

Nick shot to his feet, his hands biting into her shoulders before she could take another step.

"Don't," Caroline cried out as he dragged her toward him, the brutal grasp of his long fingers making her wince.

As she struggled his hand caught her chin, forced her face up toward him. His lips closed over hers, parting them, the fierce pressure painful. She pushed at his wide shoulders, her body writhing; then his mouth softened, warmly caressing the trembling curve of her lips, and a weak sensual need undermined her.

He moved closer, a hand sliding down her back. She was bitterly aware of the taut masculine strength of his body touching her, his thigh moving against her own, the hand on her back pressing her against him. Her heart began beating so fast that it deafened her. Unresisting, she closed her eyes and sank into a warm dark pleasure that shut off all possibility of thought.

When he lifted his head at last, she was dazed, her soft mouth trembling and bruised by the hard possession of his long kiss, and her ears were beating with the hungry roar of her own blood.

"Now tell me you didn't want me," Nick breathed in a thickened voice that was not quite steady.

She was too off balance to say a word. She looked up at him breathless, shivering, and he read the answer in her face. Her languorous green eyes spoke for her. The yielding weakness of her body as she leaned against him said that he had made his point. Caroline's quick uneven breathing made it impossible for her to speak, to deny what her body was telling him so eloquently, and Nick's mouth twisted insolently.

"Yes," he said.

Caroline's face burned with shame at the note in his voice. His fingers gripped her chin again, hurting as they bit into the delicate bones of her face.

"But I've got news for you, darling. I don't want you. Oh, you're a very sexy little blonde and I've no doubt you score with most men you fancy, but I wouldn't have you at any price. I've no intention of finding myself getting drunk to forget you. If Peter had had any guts he would have chucked you out long before you went. But you had him on his knees, so jealous he couldn't see straight, and even when he was rid of you he couldn't forget you." Nick stared into her eyes icily. "But not me, darling! You don't get me like that."

He wasn't saying anything she had not guessed he felt, but after the brief moments in his arms, when she had felt such passion flaring between them, she was shattered to have him attack her with so much violence.

Nick had never disguised the fact that he disliked and despised her, but his blue eyes and his harsh voice had made it plain just now that he detested her. Every word he had said had torn her to shreds. She wanted to get away from him, to hide, to run and keep running in order to forget, if she could, the way she had felt when he was kissing her and the way she had felt as he bit out those contemptuous phrases.

When he stared at her in silence she kept her eyes down, struggling not to start crying, fighting to keep back the words of wounded protest that he would never believe. What was the point in saying anything? He wasn't going to listen.

"Very wise," he said icily when she still stayed silent. "While you are staying in my house you will not resume your affair with Forrester. Or with anybody else. You're here simply and solely because Helen needed to see Kelly. You're not dealing with a weak fool like Peter now. If you step out of line just once, I'll slap you senseless."

Her head came up at that, outrage stiffening her. "Lay one finger on me again and I'll—"

"You'll what?" he taunted, his eyes flicking her like a lash and drawing blood.

She broke away in a desperate movement and ran to the door. She would have liked to hurt him the way he had hurt her, but for the moment the only thing that mattered was getting away from him so that she could cry in private, without Nick Holt knowing how badly he had hurt her.

In her room she sank onto the bed and buried her face in her shaking hands. She felt sick and unclean. What he had said hadn't hurt as much as how she had felt while he was holding her. It burned like poison inside her, the memory of her own hungry response, and she knew she was never going to get over it. The last time she had felt embarrassed and miserable, but this time she wanted to die; she wanted a big black hole to open up in front of her and swallow her so that she need never meet Nick Holt's scornful blue eyes again.

Every time she saw him she was going to remember, and so was he. She was living here, in the same house, and she wasn't going to be able to avoid him. Every meeting, however brief, however casual, was going to strip the skin from her and leave her feeling the way she felt now.

I hate him, she told herself. *Oh, God, what am I going to do?* She wasn't going to be able to forget this, and Nick Holt wasn't going to let her try. She couldn't go away. She had to stay, for Helen's sake, and even one more night under his roof was going to be a night in hell as far as she was concerned. How was she going to hide it?

If only I hadn't kissed him back, she thought. *If only I hadn't let myself feel like that, want him like that.* Because there was no point in hiding from that fact: she had wanted him. Her body had gone crazy as his hands touched her. She shut her eyes tight, grinding her teeth in impotent self-hatred, but that did no good. Even thinking of the encounter between them brought back that wild sweet sensation and made her ache from head to foot with remembered desire.

She had never felt like that with Peter, maybe because they had been so young. When they married she wasn't yet eighteen, and Peter was only a few years older. They had been too young to know what they were doing. *Why did we rush into it like that,* she asked herself drearily. Perhaps that was one of the reasons Peter had gone to pieces so soon: he hadn't been old enough to face the responsibilities of marriage, especially once Caroline had had Kelly. The strain had cracked him apart.

Their feelings for each other had been half imagination, half wishful thinking, as love often is when the lovers are young. Caroline looked back and knew that she hadn't known herself then, let alone been old enough to understand and know Peter.

It had all been made too easy for them. Helen had been so happy and welcoming—Caroline couldn't have had a lovelier mother-in-law if she had invented one for herself. And living with Helen had never been the sort of problem it might have been. The old music-hall jokes about mothers-in-law and sharing a house hadn't applied to them, for Caroline had loved having Helen around and Helen had been equally happy about it. It had been Peter who had become restless. Had their marriage been a disappointment to him? She would never know. She had blamed herself, as Helen had blamed herself, but to some questions there are never any answers.

She got ready for bed feeling as if she had been kicked by a horse. She knew she wouldn't sleep, but she went through the motions of putting out the light and curling up under the covers, shutting her eyes and painstakingly counting sheep.

The house was very quiet. She heard the clock in the hall strike midnight, then one. She heard the far-off whistle of a train on the line that ran between London and Scotland, and wistfully wished she was on it, heading away from Nick Holt.

SHE DIDN'T FEEL HERSELF FALLING ASLEEP, but she came awake with a vengeance, winded by the unexpected weight of Kelly on her stomach. Caroline had been sleeping on her back, her arms above her head. As her daughter landed on her she gasped, her body contracting.

"Wake up," Kelly demanded, grinning from ear to ear. "Look...."

Dazedly Caroline looked. The childish beam was comic. A little hole had appeared between the pearly teeth at the front.

"It come out," Kelly said in delight.

"Came, darling." Caroline said, wincing at the cramp in her arms. She must have slept heavily without moving for hours. The blood was surging back into her hands now that she had at last lowered her arms to her sides. She took hold of Kelly and shifted her so that she herself could sit up.

"You didn't swallow your tooth, did you?"

Kelly held out her hand. Caroline looked without pleasure at the little object.

"I'm going to put it under my pillow tonight and then I'll get a present from the tooth fairy."

"Aren't you lucky!" Caroline looked at the clock and groaned. Seven in the morning—no wonder she felt terrible! Yesterday had been an exhausting day. She had been out walking for hours and tired herself out. She should have slept like a log last night, but she had lain awake for ages. Her head throbbed and she had never felt less like getting up.

Kelly had left the door open. Suddenly someone pushed it wider.

"Anything wrong?" The deep voice at the door made Caroline's heart stop, and a cold sickness invaded her.

"Look, Uncle Nick!" Kelly said innocently, leaping off the bed and running toward the door.

Caroline's head had shot round. She saw the tall, lean-hipped figure in a silk dressing gown, caught the sardonic smile and pulled the bedclothes over her—but not quickly enough.

"Oh, your tooth's gone, has it?" Nick said. "Congratulations. Now you'll be able to whistle."

Kelly chattered to him in the doorway while Caroline longed to scream at him to get out of her room. The brief all-seeing look he had flung her had left her skin burning everywhere he had observed it, as though he had touched rather than looked.

He went and Kelly came back to ask, "When are you getting up, mummy? Can we have breakfast, mummy? I'm hungry! Are you hungry, mummy? I could eat a horse! Uncle Nick is up, mummy. Why don't you get up, mummy?"

She had never felt like screaming at Kelly before. Usually she had patience with her. Usually she let the unceasing chatter flow over her while she cooked, cleaned, got her daughter ready for school.

She swallowed the impulse to scream and said, "Why don't you go and wash, darling? Then you can get dressed and we'll go down for breakfast." But not until Nick had gone, she thought. Somehow she would have to delay Kelly until he was out of the house and there was no danger of running into him.

"I washed," Kelly said, but she looked guilty.

Caroline warned, "Kelly, don't tell fibs."

"Well, I'm clean," Kelly insisted. "And I'm not going to school. . . ." She met her mother's gaze and said with that gap-toothed grin, "I'll go and wash."

Caroline laughed as her daughter vanished. Sometimes it had bothered her that Kelly had to go without male influence. She told herself that after the sort of unreasoning, unpredictable violence the child had known from her father, the last thing she needed was physical discipline, but she had a nagging doubt. She never slapped Kelly. She tried to guide her by gentle firmness rather than by that discipline, and although she kept telling herself it was the right way to bring her daughter up, she had doubts from time to time, usually when she ran into some problem with her. So far, however, Kelly seemed to respond to that gentle guidance.

This morning was the first time Caroline had ever had to fight to make herself stay patient with Kelly. She had been so absorbed in the pain of remembering last night that she hadn't had any energy to spare.

She made a firm resolution. *I will not think about him today. I will not even let him cross my mind.*

That was easier said than done, of course. She took her time in the bathroom while Kelly danced about outside, hissing through the door, "How long will you be? I'm hungry, mummy. Will you be long?"

Caroline told her to wait in the bedroom and did not hurry herself, despite Kelly's long-suffering sighs. She put on a cherry red sweater and well-washed blue jeans before she joined her daughter, who gave her a sulky glare. "Uncle Nick's gone now. I heard his car."

"Oh, dear," Caroline said blithely, taking her hand. "Never mind." Thank God for that, she thought. She could not have sat down at the breakfast table with those blue eyes flicking over her.

Mrs. Bentall told them with gloomy satisfaction that the news was bad. "Air crash in Bolivia, earthquake in Mexico, and they say it will be a bad winter here."

Caroline bit her lip. "Oh, dear," she said, hoping her amusement didn't show.

"Bacon and eggs all right?" Mrs. Bentall looked at Kelly, who was eating porridge with concentration. "What about you, Kelly?"

Kelly nodded and Caroline said, "I'm sure Kelly would love bacon and eggs, but I'm not very hungry, Mrs. Bentall. Could I have just a slice of toast?"

"Have what you like," Mrs. Bentall said, stalking to the door with an offended look.

Kelly had finished her porridge. She sat back, beaming. "She can't abide people who waste good food," she told her mother.

"Mrs. Bentall can't?"

Kelly nodded. "When I couldn't eat my supper last night because I was so full up with jam tarts, she said starving Indian peasants would have been glad of it and I should be thankful to get a crust."

"So you should," Caroline agreed.

"Uncle Nick wastes good food," Kelly told her.

Caroline looked at her sharply. "Does he? Why?"

"Works all the hours God sends and you can't be sure he'll come in at the proper time for his meals." Kelly had an almost word-perfect memory and could mimic other people without thinking about it. She had suddenly acquired a broad Yorkshire accent. Even her small face had taken on Mrs. Bentall's dry expression. "That man needs to be spoken to, but he'll not listen," she went on. "She said Uncle Nick was wicked, mummy," she added with rounded eyes. "Is he? Is he really wicked, mummy?"

Caroline couldn't imagine what Mrs. Bentall had meant. "I'm sure she didn't mean that."

"She did; she said he had a wicked temper and he was wickedly obstinate into the bargain. What does she mean, mummy?"

"I've no idea," Caroline said dryly. Oh, no, not much, she thought. Mrs. Bentall knew the man, obviously.

The door was pushed open and the housekeeper

came in carrying a tray. She sniffed as she handed Caroline her toast, but gave Kelly an approving look, placing the cooked breakfast in front of her.

The morning was dry and sunny again, the light above the moorlands on the horizon a delicate primrose color. After breakfast Helen got up and decided she felt well enough to take a short walk around the garden. Caroline went with her and they paused to look across the open rolling moors. The air was crisp and scented with autumn.

"We don't tell ourselves often enough how good it is to be alive," Helen said suddenly, smiling at her, and as Caroline smiled back she told herself that however badly Nick thought of her, it was worth the humiliation and pain of living in his house for a while just to see Helen smile like that again.

CHAPTER FIVE

HER NERVES BEGAN TO TIGHTEN as the day wore on, and she began to count the minutes apprehensively, watching the clock. She did not know how she was going to put up with having Nick look at her with that biting hostility, and she had a hard struggle hiding her state of mind from Helen. It was an enormous relief when Mrs. Bentall came in at six to say that Nick wouldn't be coming home that evening.

"Working late," the housekeeper said glumly. "As usual. He ought to slow up a bit before he blows a fuse. What does he think he is—a machine?"

When she had gone Helen sighed. "She's right. Nick does work far too hard, but then he does have problems. This world recession hits everybody. Nick says he has to work twice as hard to stay still. He has to fight like mad for every sale."

Caroline hardly heard her. She was bathed in tired relief because she wasn't going to have to face him that evening.

She and Helen had dinner alone. Frey rang to ask if Helen was okay and promised to call in if he had time the next day. He was busy, too; his partner had come down with flu and was in bed, so Frey was doing both rounds.

At nine-thirty Helen got up and said she was going to bed. She looked at the fire, which was blazing up the chimney, and Caroline promised to deal with it before she herself followed upstairs.

The two golden Labradors lay on the hearth, their noses on their paws, twitching slightly as they slept. Caroline began to damp down the fire for the night, her mind occupied with worrying about Helen and the future. She had explored every idea that came to her, but she was nervously aware of flaws in all of them.

She turned toward the door, sighing, and heard a car engine throbbing on the driveway. It cut out and a door slammed. The dogs began to bark and Caroline hurried to reach the stairs before Nick got into the house. The dogs came with her, barking, tails wagging, and she shushed them, frowning. They would wake the whole house with that racket.

The door flew open. The wind rushed into the house, bringing Nick with it, and the dogs flew at him, clambering up his long lean form to give him an eager welcome. He pushed them down, grinning, then shot a look at Caroline, who had frozen halfway across the hall.

She watched the long fingers as he played with the golden coats. With dogs, as with Kelly, Nick was gentle.

"Good night," she said, and walked toward the stairs.

"Did Mrs. Bentall leave me any supper?" he asked casually, and she looked over her shoulder.

"I've no idea. She went off to her little flat after

dinner. If she left you anything, I imagine it's in the kitchen."

He ran a hand over his face in a tired gesture. "I'm knocked out and I'm starving. I haven't eaten since lunchtime."

"You can't work on an empty stomach," Caroline said, slowly turning around.

"I work best on an empty stomach," Nick responded dryly. "It concentrates the mind."

Caroline hesitated. "I'll see if Mrs. Bentall left anything for you," she offered, since he appeared to be incapable of doing anything but lean against the door in a weary attitude, scratching the heads of the dogs in a lazy way.

"Thanks," he said calmly, and she had no choice but to walk into the kitchen. He followed in a moment after shutting the dogs into the sitting room.

"I can't find anything," she said, turning to look at him. "Would you like sandwiches? Or eggs and bacon?"

"Sandwiches would be fine," Nick said, yawning, his hands crossed on top of his head and his long body stretched to its full length. She watched the relaxed lines of his face, the thick lashes moving against his cheek, and she looked away, her heart beating fast.

He watched her make some coffee and a little pile of cold-beef sandwiches, and the silence in the kitchen beat against her nerves until she thought she would scream. Nick didn't take his eyes off her and she began to feel like a rabbit being watched by a snake, trapped in a feeling of fascination, fear, hypnotized passivity.

She searched her mind for something neutral to talk

about. Before Peter began to poison Nick's mind against her, they had had a friendly relationship. It seemed a long time ago, another world, another time, but it had existed and they must have talked about something. They hadn't hurled angry words at each other then. What had they discussed?

Brightly she began, "Helen tells me your firm is going through a bad patch."

Nick shrugged. "I wouldn't say that, exactly. The firm is doing fine—it's just harder to sell our goods these days. We have to go out and fight for every sale."

"You work very long hours, don't you?" She switched off the percolator and got out a cup and saucer for him.

"At the moment I've no choice."

She poured him a cup of coffee while he watched her in that brooding way, and she angrily asked herself why she let him get to her. In sheer self-protection she ought to be able to ignore the constant surveillance of those hard blue eyes, but fight as she could, she was powerless to make herself unaware of him.

"You ought to relax more," she told him, and his mouth twisted in dry amusement.

"Is that an invitation?"

She knew she flushed, and hated herself. She put the plate of sandwiches in front of him and turned toward the door without answering. Nick stood up and caught her shoulders, pulling her backward so that she rested against his long body. She shivered as she felt his mouth moving against her hair.

"I take that back," he said huskily. "I'm too tired to think straight tonight."

"You shouldn't work so hard," she whispered, deeply aware of him and wishing he would let her go. "And don't try to think. Eat your supper and go to bed, Nick. You can't keep working at this rate or you'll crack up."

"Maybe I have," he muttered, massaging the slender curve of her shoulder, his fingers warm and sensitive as they stroked along her collarbone. "I must be crazy. Sometimes I tell myself to stop thinking, too, and just take what I want."

Her heart turned over inside her and her breath caught, the little gasp audible.

His fingers tightened for a second, then pushed her away, almost as if he were afraid of what he might do.

"Go to bed, Caroline," he said in a low deep voice. "Before I forget all the reasons why I would need to be insane to get involved with you."

He turned away and Caroline walked unsteadily out of the room, her face pale now.

SHE SLEPT BADLY again that night. When she got up she was still tired, and to wake herself up she took the dogs for a walk across the moors. Helen smiled at her as she met her later, looking approvingly at her wind-flushed cheeks.

"You look very healthy," she said, and Caroline smiled wryly.

Frey called in that afternoon and spent ten minutes talking to them, his gray eyes observing Helen meticulously all the time.

"How do you think she is today?" Caroline asked as she walked with him to his car.

"Looking much better. You and Kelly are doing more than any medicine could. Keep it up."

Caroline sighed. "We can only stay about a week."

Frey halted and studied her face. "Can't you make it longer than that?"

"Not really. I've got a job to go back to, remember?"

"Caroline, if you had seen Helen a fortnight ago you would realize just what you and Kelly have done for her. If you go away again I can't be responsible for what might happen." He spoke in a low flat voice and with long pauses between the words, as though searching for the right thing to say, and Caroline's heart sank.

"Oh," she said, because there was nothing else to say.

Frey took her hand and squeezed it. "Think about what I've said. We all need something to live for. You and Kelly are the only reasons Helen has."

He drove away, and Caroline stared at the blue autumn sky. What should she do? Frey had just landed her fairly and squarely with the responsibility of keeping Helen alive. He knew what he had done. He had spoken with calm deliberation, although his gray eyes had been gentle. Caroline wished she could tell herself that Frey was exaggerating, but she had a feeling he wasn't. She had felt it that first day when Helen looked at her granddaughter with painful eagerness.

She had several alternatives. She could either find a larger house and keep her job in London, or give up her job and come back to Skeldale. Or possibly she could share her bedroom with Kelly for a while and have a small extension built onto the back of the bungalow. There was just about room, although it would leave them with a much smaller garden.

That evening, after Kelly had gone to bed, she broached the subject to Helen, who listened with a faint sigh.

"Oh, dear, I didn't want to think about the future," she said revealingly.

"We must," Caroline said, taking both her hands. "There's no hurry to make up your mind, but we ought to talk it over."

"I can't land myself on you," Helen said, and Caroline shook her head at her.

"There's no question of landing yourself. We want you, both Kelly and I. How could we leave you here in Skeldale alone?"

"I don't know if I could live in London," Helen said, and as she spoke Nick walked into the room and stopped short, staring at them.

"Live in London?" he repeated. "Of course you couldn't! What pin brain brought that idea up?"

Bristling, Caroline said, "I did," and he gave her a dismissive stare.

"I might have known."

"It's very kind of Caroline—" Helen began.

"Taking you away from the place you've lived in for sixty years? You call that kind, do you?" Nick demanded, and Caroline's face flushed.

"Caroline has such a good job," Helen said hurriedly, seeing the stormy look in Caroline's green eyes. "I couldn't ask her to give that up for me. She'd never get such a good job in Skeldale."

His mouth twisted grimly. "Thinking up new ways of selling women things they don't need? Churning out slogans for soap flakes and suntan oil—oh, yes, we wouldn't want to deprive her of such a world-shattering experience, would we?"

"Oh, you think you're so damned funny!" burst out Caroline. "I've had enough of your snide digs about me. It's none of your business!"

"I'm making it my business," he told her with biting emphasis.

"Like hell you are," she said, and Helen looked aghast, staring from one to the other of them. Perhaps she hadn't noticed the enmity between them before, but she was noticing it now, and worry was etching lines across her forehead.

"Helen belongs in Skeldale and she's staying. What would she do in some ugly little London suburb, all alone in a tiny bungalow all day while you're at work and Kelly's at school? All the people she knows live here, all the places she cares about are here, and you aren't tearing her up by the roots and carting her off to a strange place just to suit yourself!"

Helen made little noises of distress, but Caroline was too angry to notice them. She glared at Nick, her color high, her eyes fierce. He had put into words what she had secretly been aware of herself, but she did not thank him for it. She hated him for it. He had stripped her of alternatives and left her facing the fact that she had no choice at all.

The sardonic blue eyes enforced what he had just said, noting with satisfaction that Caroline seemed speechless. Then he added dryly, "As for a job, you can have one with us. I was thinking it was time we started a publicity department. I've been using free-lance firms, but it's time we had our own people.''

She dumbly shook her head, too staggered to answer. Work for him? See him every day? Not in a million years!

"What a wonderful idea, Nick!" Helen said excitedly. "Caroline would be her own boss, wouldn't she? It would be a great opportunity for her."

No, thought Caroline drowningly, looking at her mother-in-law with dazed green eyes.

"The air here would be so much better for Kelly than all the petrol fumes and smoke you get in London," Helen said. "I'm sure she would be much happier in a smaller school, too. Those huge London schools never have the same happy atmosphere as a school in a small town."

Nick had been watching Caroline with comprehending mockery. She met his eyes with a sinking heart.

"It's so kind of you, Nick," Helen said. "I'm sure Caroline will be marvelous at the job. After all, she's had a good training. She'll find it very exciting to put her own ideas into practice."

If Caroline knew Nick Holt, the only ideas being put into practice would come from his head, and she would rapidly find herself being reduced to taking orders morning, noon and night. *Never,* she thought, letting Helen's excited words wash over her head. *I couldn't take it.* After another week of having Nick look at her the way he did now, she would be ready to jump out of a window.

"That's settled, then," Nick said.

Caroline's head jerked up. She met his eyes and got a mocking little smile before he strode to the door and went out.

Helen looked at her with faint anxiety. "You do like the idea, don't you? It's up to you, dear, of course. You must do whatever you think is best for you and Kelly, but I do think she would be much better off in Skeldale than she is in a London suburb."

Caroline forced a smile. "You may be right."

"Oh, I'm sure I am. Everything is so impersonal in London suburbs, isn't it? People don't talk to each other the way we do here, not even in shops. They don't seem to have time to bother with you. Now if I go into my butcher's he always takes the time to chat to me. You feel at home here. I've never lived in London, but I don't get the feeling that anyone there feels at home."

"It depends on what you're used to," Caroline said.

Helen bit her lip. "Well, I don't want to press you, dear...."

Caroline smiled at her. "It would solve a lot of problems," she made herself say, because Helen was looking disappointed and she didn't want to hurt her. "I'll think about it for a day or two," she added, and Helen sighed, nodding.

Detaching herself from Helen with a muttered excuse, she went upstairs to change, and met Nick coming down. He paused, eyeing her mockingly, but did not step aside to let her pass, standing a stair above her so that she had to look up at him, her skin heating as she met the insolent stare of the blue eyes.

To her surprise he was in evening dress, the wide

shoulders under the immaculately tailored jacket emphasizing his long lean body, his tanned skin throwing the crisp white shirt into prominence. He looked fantastic, and that made her angrier than ever.

"You haven't thanked me," he drawled.

"For what?" The words were spat out of her like bullets, but that only seemed to amuse him more.

"The offer of a job."

"I haven't made up my mind whether I want it yet. I don't know if I want to work in Skeldale."

He shrugged. "Employment prospects in Skeldale are thin on the ground."

"I can always go farther afield."

"York?" he murmured, his mouth a wry line. "Yes, I suppose you could get a job there, but it would mean a very long journey to work each day and Kelly wouldn't see much of you."

That was true, but she met his gaze with irritated eyes. He seemed taller than ever, looking down at her from the upper stair, his air of mocking relaxation deliberately intended to make her feel at a disadvantage.

"Your manners leave a lot to be desired," he murmured, and she set her teeth, bristling.

"My manners?"

"You still haven't said thank-you," he pointed out, lowering his black lashes and eyeing her through them.

"Thank you." The words had the force and point of a knife, and her green eyes were filled with hatred.

"You don't sound too sincere," he mocked.

Caroline trembled with rage. "My feelings are very

real," she muttered through her teeth, wanting to slap him across his smiling face.

"If I weren't in a hurry I'd explore that subject with fascination," he informed, her glancing at his watch. "We'll have to postpone the discussion for some more convenient moment."

"Drop dead," she hissed, shaking, her hands clenched at her sides, and he laughed silkily. But as his lashes shifted and she met the full brilliance of the hard blue eyes, there was an unveiled threat in them from which she wanted to run and never stop running.

"Don't hurry to make up your mind about the job," he said. "I can wait. I'll wait till doomsday if I have to."

A chill ran down her spine. That had not been lightly said. It reinforced the threat in the blue eyes and made her feel bitterly afraid.

He drew aside to let her pass and she hurried up the stairs, beset by waves of cold panic. She had an uneasy suspicion that she was not going to find any other job in Skeldale. It was a very small town, and as he had said, jobs were rare, especially jobs that provided a good salary. Nick had known very well that his offer was one she was going to find hard to refuse.

Behind those vivid blue eyes was a hard, calculating mind, she decided. He thought he had her trapped. The most disturbing part of the situation was that he probably did, and Caroline was painfully aware that if she took a job with Nick's firm she was going to find herself being put through a wringer. The smile he had given her as he stood aside had been triumphant.

When she returned downstairs Helen told her that

Nick had gone to a dinner party. "With the Skeltons," she added, sighing.

Caroline's brows met. "I don't remember them."

"You wouldn't, dear; they moved here a year ago. Henry Skelton was a manufacturer in Africa somewhere. He retired and came home and invested some of his capital in Nick's firm. Nick sees quite a bit of them."

"Where do they live?" Caroline searched her mind for the sort of house a wealthy man might choose around Skeldale, but such houses were few and far between. Nick had one of the few large houses in the district.

"Below Hougham," Helen said.

Frowning, Caroline murmured, "I don't remember any houses there." It was a quiet stretch of moorland, as she recalled it, looking down over the town.

"They built one. Don't you remember the lower pasture Joe Bond used to graze his horses on? He sold it to Henry Skelton."

"Oh, what a pity! That must have spoiled the view of Hougham Tor."

"It did, dear, but I believe Joe got a very good price for it, and it *is* true that it wasn't a very good piece of land. He couldn't grow anything on it; the soil was too thin and there was too much rock embedded in it. He did try, he said, during the war, but he gave up when he kept turning up huge rocks with his plow. The council gave permission for the change of use and Skelton got his house."

"Is it nice?"

Helen made a face. "Very modern. I don't care for

it myself, but they say it is well designed and full of up-to-date gadgets. Mrs. Bentall's cousin Ruby works there and she is always boasting about her kitchen. Hazel Skelton had a kitchen designer down from London, she says, and apparently it is like something out of *Star Wars*."

"Hazel Skelton is the wife?"

"Daughter," Helen said. "Quite striking to look at, but I can't say I was very impressed by her manners. I was introduced to her at a party here the Christmas they arrived and she shook hands, said two words to me and then walked away. Half an hour later someone introduced me again and before I could say yes, we had met, she went through the same process again. She didn't even remember me and I don't suppose she does now."

Caroline laughed. "Charming girl!"

"That's what I thought, dear, but Nick sees quite a lot of her."

Caroline went on smiling. "Oh, does he? Maybe they have something in common." It sounded as if they had a lot in common, she thought.

Later that evening Helen said, "Why don't we sell the old house, dear, and find somewhere more modern, a new place for a new start? I think we would all feel much happier somewhere else, don't you?"

There was a split-second pause as Caroline faced the fact that this was the moment of choice, but then what choice did she have? She could not walk out on Helen, and Nick was right: she couldn't remove her from Skeldale after sixty years there.

"Up to you," she answered brightly, and hoped

Helen hadn't noticed that tiny moment of hesitation. "I'm happy to do whatever you want."

"I think it would be best," Helen said, smiling with a tremulous relief. Yes, she had noticed the second's doubt. "Kelly would certainly be much happier in a different house. It really would be a fresh start for all of us."

Caroline nodded.

"And you *will* take Nick's job? I think it is a marvelous opportunity for you," Helen went on with enthusiasm.

Caroline swallowed. "Yes, I'll take it," she told her with a sense of grim foreboding.

Helen kissed her cheek, patted her hand. "I'm glad," she said in a rough husky voice. "Thank you, my dear."

In her bed later Caroline sat staring at the tiny gray moth fluttering desperately around the lampshade, powdery wings beating as it flung itself, infatuated, at the light, only to be driven away by the heat of the glass bulb. Repeatedly it fluttered off and came back again, unable to tear itself away. She knew precisely how it felt.

Nothing would please her more than to get away from there and know she need never see Nick again, but she couldn't do that to Helen. She was held fast to Skeldale by ties of affection, duty and regret. She had abandoned Helen and run away last time, and although she had made plenty of excuses for herself that had sounded good to her at the time, she had always felt guilty about it. She had to make some amends now.

Helen had gone through so much that Caroline couldn't walk out on her again. This time she had no excuses and her own fondness for Helen wouldn't allow her to go, but she knew without needing to be told openly by Nick that he would take every opportunity he got to hurt her and humiliate her. He believed she deserved that. He believed she was all the things Peter had claimed she was, and she had no way of proving those claims false. She was going to have to live with Nick's contempt and deliberate needling, and it was not going to be a very pleasant experience.

OVER BREAKFAST the next day she discussed her plans with Kelly gently, feeling her way into the subject.

"Live in Skeldale?" Kelly's amber eyes opened wide. "Forever, mummy?"

"Forever is a long time. Certainly for the next few years," Caroline told her, watching her closely. She was not sure how Kelly would react, and if her daughter showed signs of emotional stress she was going to have a problem on her hands. Kelly had been badly frightened by Peter during her early years; her memories of Skeldale were not happy ones. Caroline just did not know how the child would feel.

Kelly dipped a finger of bread and butter into her boiled egg and nibbled at it, her brows set in a frown.

"How do you feel about the idea?" Caroline asked.

"What about our house?"

"We would sell that."

"I wouldn't see Sharon ever again," Kelly said gloomily.

"She could come and stay with us. Think what fun it would be showing her the moors."

"What would Miss Oldham say?" Kelly was in great awe of her class teacher, who seemed to her to be a close relation of God.

"She would miss you, but if we stay in London grandma will miss you much more." Caroline did not want to thrust the burden of emotional responsibility for Helen onto Kelly's small shoulders, but she knew she had to point out that aspect of the situation to her gently.

Kelly stared at her plate. "Would we live in grandma's house?"

Caroline thought of the painting she had hanging on her wall in the bungalow, the house with black windows and a shadow reaching out toward running figures.

She winced. "No. Grandma is going to sell it and buy a new one. You can help us choose it."

The door opened and Nick strode into the room. It was a Saturday and he had not gone to work, she realized. She had somehow imagined that he had, since there had been no sign of him, and now she started, her green eyes wide as they flew to his face.

Kelly welcomed him with excitement. "Hello, Uncle Nick, guess what? Grandma is going to sell her house and we're going to live here forever!"

Over the child's brown head Caroline met Nick's satisfied gaze and looked away.

Mrs. Bentall took Kelly off to the kitchen five minutes later—to help her, she said, winking at Caroline behind the little girl's back—and when they had gone Caroline hurriedly got up from the table to escape the dangerous proximity of Nick's brooding presence on the other side of it.

"Where are you going?" he demanded, his black head lifting from his perusal of the morning paper.

"I thought. . . ."

"Sit down," he said tersely.

"I have a lot to do." Caroline resented the way he talked to her and she wasn't putting up with it much longer, particularly in view of the fact that she was going to have to work with him sometime in the future, and if he continued to treat her with that cutting disdain life was sure to be impossible.

"Sit down," he repeated. "I want to talk to you." He folded the paper and put it down, leaning back in his chair.

Reluctantly she sat. "Well?"

"I take it you are accepting my offer of a job?"

Her face was very pale, her green eyes hectic against the pallor of her skin. She would have loved to say no, facing him out, but she was helpless in the grip of circumstances and he knew it. She couldn't find the courage to say so aloud, though, her back very straight, her chin up in bitter defiance.

He watched her intently, the power in his lean body vibrating almost visibly as he enjoyed her helpless inability to do anything but accept.

"Yes or no?" he asked coolly.

She moistened her trembling lips. "Yes," she whispered.

"I can't hear you." He was smiling, and she hated him so much she wanted to throw things at him.

"Liar," she muttered in a low husky voice. "You heard me. You didn't need to hear. You knew I was going to accept. I haven't any alternative, have I?"

"None," he said with silky satisfaction, his blue eyes narrowed and closely observant. "So we can discuss terms now, can we?"

"Terms?" The word sank into her and she stiffened. What did that mean? She looked at him, pupils dilating, and he grinned at her.

"It's customary," he drawled.

She searched his hard face, trying to work out exactly what he meant, afraid to consider what could lie behind the word.

"Is it?"

"Surely," he murmured, his mouth curling upward at the edges and the blue eyes wickedly amused. "We haven't discussed salary, for a start, or working hours."

Caroline's involuntary sigh of relief amused him even more, and she glared at him. He had known she was alarmed by what he had said and he had been deliberately teasing her, making her afraid that he was about to make her some sort of proposition. It hadn't been so much the word "terms" as the insolent appraisal of the blue eyes as they moved over her from her honey-blond hair down past the warm curves of her body, lingering possessively in a way that made her feel weak and stricken.

"This morning you can come out to the factory and look at the office space I'm going to give you," he told her. "We can discuss terms of employment there. It will be a better atmosphere."

"I have to give notice and work out a full month," she pointed out. "My firm will need to find a replacement."

"No hurry," he nodded. "There will be a good deal to arrange before you get to work for me, anyway. At present the office I plan to turn into a publicity department is being used as a storeroom. It will have to be redesigned and furnished, and that will take time." He stood up, towering over her. "We might as well go over now and take a look at it."

Caroline slowly stood up. He watched her, an enigmatic look in his eyes, and she told herself that she was going to have to learn to hide her feelings from him. She would never be able to work with Nick Holt around if those insolent eyes could always pierce through her head and read her mind. She would give anything to be indifferent to him, to be able to ignore the taunting smiles and contemptuous remarks; but failing that, she was going to have to learn to pretend an indifference she could not feel, or he would make her life a permanent purgatory.

CHAPTER SIX

IT WAS SIX WEEKS before she started work at the factory. She had returned to London and broken the news to Grey a few days after visiting the office that Nick had chosen for the new publicity department. Grey had been furious when she told him her decision and had spent some time trying to argue her out of it, pointing out, with a great deal of justice, that he had given her a marvelous opportunity when he appointed her as a copywriter and that she owed him some loyalty and consideration. He was very persuasive, a man with a genius for using words as weapons, and he made her feel small and mean as he roared his fury at her.

"Where is this place, anyway? I never heard of it. Out at the back of beyond! Some twopenny, half-penny firm that'll pay you in buttons—are you crazy? You'll never get anywhere with an outfit like that. Who's heard of them? London is where you need to be, especially now, when you're right on the bottom rung of the business. Skeldale—where the hell is that?" Grey had never heard of anywhere past Watford and imagined the rest of England was inhabited by men in bearskins and woad. For him the world was bounded by the London suburbs. He never went into *them*, either, if he could help it.

"I'm sorry, Grey! I'm very grateful to you...."

"So I should damned well think! I must have had a hole in my head, giving you that job in the first place." He was looking very sulky, his bland smile absent.

"But this is nothing to do with my career—"

"What career? You're hellbent on chucking that away!"

"This is a family obligation," Caroline said, and he looked at her in complete bafflement. Grey did not recognize such concepts. He was a clever, sophisticated man who had no room in his life for anything but work.

"Caroline, you're nuts," he said.

"I know. I'm sorry," Caroline said, stifling a smile.

"Family obligation," he grunted incredulously, and shook his head.

"Don't you have a family?" From the amazed way he stared at her when she asked that, she got the impression Grey had not been born so much as designed and built to be launched upon the world as a one-man army of conquest. He had dedicated his life to the agency. He meant to claw to the top in his chosen sphere, and nothing would ever get in his way and push him back into mediocrity. *Success* was the only word he wanted to hear.

"I've got to do this," she said quietly, and Grey gave up the struggle, seeing she was not going to be moved.

"You're a stupid, obstinate fool," he told her bitterly. "Giving up your career for some old lady! For a man, I could understand, but an old lady? That's nutty!"

"It's because she's old that I have to do it," Caroline pointed out. "Kelly and I are all the family she has, and she's too old to come all the way to London."

"Well, go then," Grey bellowed, slamming out of the office, but before she left he softened enough to wish her luck and tell her that if she ever needed a job to get in touch. "I might—just might, mind you—give you one," he said, grimacing. "After I've had a shrink look at you. If ever I saw someone who was due for a session with a psychiatrist it's you, but you're a bright kid on your good days and I'll be sorry to lose you."

"I'm sorry to go," she said wistfully, and she was even more sorry that she was going to be working with Nick Holt in the future. For all his insistence on success, Grey was a good boss and a man she liked.

It was even harder to face saying goodbye to her little bungalow and the family next door. Sharon was in floods of tears, swapping toys with Kelly as she watched her pack, begging Kelly to write to her and promising to come and visit at Skeldale.

Deirdre was stricken, too. She and Caroline had become close friends during the eighteen months they had lived next door to each other. Deirdre was only partly comforted when Caroline sold the bungalow almost at once to a lively family with three children, whose mother seemed both pleasant and friendly.

"It won't be the same," Deirdre said gloomily. "I'll miss you."

"You'll come and visit us, won't you? You'll like Skeldale."

"Frankly, I hate the place," Deirdre said, smiling

slightly. "It has snatched you both away and I'm going to be anti-Skeldale for a long time."

Kelly was crying as they drove away in the taxi that had come to take them to the station. Caroline put an arm around her and hugged her comfortingly. "Never mind, you'll see Sharon soon."

"Not soon," Kelly sobbed. "Not for ages." She lifted tearstained eyes and wailed, "And I bet I'll never see Miss Oldham again!"

Caroline was silenced. Personally, she couldn't find that a terrible prospect, since Miss Oldham had a face like an old spoon and a ferocious grimace that passed for a smile, but it was obvious that Kelly thought otherwise. At this moment her daughter could see no ray of sunshine in the world.

At seven, though, life moves with the speed of light. By the time they were back in Skeldale, Kelly was jogging up and down excitedly in anticipation of seeing Nick.

"I wonder if he'll meet us? I wonder if he'll fetch us in his car?"

"We can take a taxi from the station." Caroline hoped Nick would not meet them, but when Kelly tumbled out of the compartment she gave a squeal of joy and ran off calling, "Uncle Nick, Uncle Nick, we're here, we're here!"

Caroline slowly followed her out of the train. Nick's strong fingers seized her cases and she looked up warily at the hard blue eyes as they flashed over her.

"Had a good journey?"

"Yes, thank you," she said in a polite voice, looking away from that mocking expression.

"The car's outside." He walked away and Kelly danced beside him, chattering. Caroline followed in their wake, watching as her daughter gazed up at Nick, watching his bent head and amused, attentive smile.

"Helen's still staying with me," he told her as they drove away from the railway station.

Caroline went rigid. "I thought she would have gone back to her own house by now."

"I decided that was a bad idea," he drawled.

"*You* decided?" Her voice came sharply, but she was not surprised to hear that.

He gave her a sardonic look. "That's right. Helen didn't want to go back there and I can't blame her. The house is full of unhappy memories...." His voice cut off, dropping as he ended that remark, and he looked back quickly at Kelly, who was gazing out of the window. It was impossible to tell from her face whether she had heard or not.

Caroline sighed. He was right, of course. The house was full of unhappy memories for them all and she had been dreading the idea of going back there. Kelly hadn't said a word about it. Caroline had a suspicion that Kelly imagined they were going back to Nick's house, anyway. It hadn't entered her head, perhaps, that they would be going anywhere else.

When they got to the house Kelly flew ahead to find her grandmother. Caroline and Nick joined them and found Helen talking to Frey, who looked up with a smile of pleasure.

"Caroline, wonderful to see you back and even more wonderful that you're here to stay."

"Thanks," she said, kissing Helen. She gave her

mother-in-law a rapid survey and was relieved to see that there had been a definite change for the better. "You look much more like yourself," she told her, and Helen looked pleased.

"Thanks to this man," she said, patting Frey's hand.

Nick moved to the door, his expression wry. Caroline looked after him, frowning. Nick had done so much for Helen, too. He had given her a home, found Caroline and Kelly, shown Helen endless kindness. She looked back at her mother-in-law and Helen was laughing as Kelly poured out a long account of the train journey.

"I must be off," Frey said. "Walk with me to my car, Caroline?"

"Yes, do, dear," Helen said eagerly.

Caroline walked out with Frey, her brow creased. Frey glanced at her inquiringly, one brow lifted.

"Something wrong?"

"Not really," she said, her brow clearing. Helen was very fond of Frey and she was perceptive in her judgment. Frey was a good man, a kind, hardworking, thoughtful man who didn't spare himself for the people in his care. He cared about Helen and he had tried patiently to help Peter. Caroline couldn't recall Frey's ever making a single critical remark about Peter. He had seen and understood without passing judgment, and that was a rare human ability.

"You aren't regretting giving up your job and your London world?" Frey asked, watching her.

She shook her head. "It was inevitable, and you know, I think it will be a better life for Kelly here."

"I'm sure it will," Grey agreed. "And for you, too."

Caroline laughed. "Oh, me!"

"Yes, you," he said. "Don't you matter?"

Caroline pretended to consider that, her face wry. "If I ever have time to think about it, I'll tell you."

"Think about it now," he prompted, smiling. In the soft dusky twilight his face looked younger, less lined, less tired. Daylight was cruel to human faces. It picked out every wrinkle, every passing expression.

"Kelly is very important to me," she said. "If she is happy I'll be happy."

"Caroline, you can't live your life through Kelly forever. You're a loving mother, but sometime soon you're going to have to start living for yourself."

Startled, she looked up, her green eyes wide. "Don't be absurd. I don't live my life through Kelly, but she's my child; I have to take care of her, make sure she is well and happy. She's my responsibility—she always has been."

"She's your responsibility, but she's not your life, Caroline," he said, getting into his car. He wound down the window and smiled up at her. "The minute she's an adult she is going to walk away; that's what being an adult means. That's the end you're working toward, whether you know it or not: turning Kelly into a self-sufficient, responsible adult. And then what? What about you then?"

Caroline stared at him blankly. "That's years away."

"Exactly," he said, starting the engine. "Years of your life." He gave her a wave and the car drove off, leaving her staring after it in fixed puzzlement. Giving herself a little shake, she went back into the house and straight into Nick, whose hands gripped her arms to steady her as she tripped. The bite of his fingers was painful and she looked up in instinctive protest to meet savage contempt in his eyes.

"Stay away from Forrester," he grated in a low harsh tone meant only for her ears and not intended to be heard by Kelly and Helen in the far room. "I didn't bring you back here for him. You aren't waltzing back into his life and taking up where you left off, Caroline. I won't let you get off that easily."

Her face paled. "What are you talking about? What right do you have to talk to me like that?"

"Did you think I'd forget all you did to my cousin?" The cruel tightness of his fingers intensified and he shook her, her bright blond head flung back and forth as if she were a rag doll. Nick bent toward her, speaking through his almost closed lips, his voice only just audible, his blue eyes eating her. "Payoff time always comes in the end, Caroline, however hard and fast you run, and your running days are over. I've got you and I intend to keep you right under my eye, and you're going to pay for what you did to Peter; you're going to pay for every hour of misery you gave him!"

She listened with rising fear, her face quite white now, her eyes enormous as they stared up at his.

"You're wrong," she managed to stammer at last.

His mouth writhed in icy mimicry of a smile. "Don't start that again. We both know I'm not wrong. You're an amoral, promiscuous little bitch without either heart or conscience, but I'm going to teach you a few well-deserved lessons." The blue eyes were glittering fiercely. "Starting now."

His hands shot up to clasp her face, tilting it back. Off balance, she caught hold of him to steady herself, giving a low gasp of fear. The gasp was silenced as Nick's mouth brutally imposed itself upon hers. Caroline's hands curled helplessly, electricity sending a current of intense pain and excitement along her veins. She swayed weakly against him, moaning under the force of his kiss, and through his shirt she felt the warmth of his strong body, the rapid tattoo of his heart racing against her own tumultuous heartbeat.

Her hands slowly slid around his neck and up into his thick black hair. The vital strands clung to her skin. She was lying against him, shuddering, aware of that lean muscular body in every nerve, every cell. She could not break free, either physically or emotionally. She was helpless in the clutch of a spiraling sexual desire she had suppressed for so long that it had the violence of a bursting dam as it poured through her.

Nick lifted his head, breathing thickly, his chest heaving as though he had been running for his life.

Caroline was still clinging to him, her arms around his neck, her body throbbing in a sensual compulsion that she had been trying to deny to herself ever since she'd seen him again, and when she opened her drowsy green eyes Nick looked into them with fixed intensity.

His skin was darkly flushed. He looked from her eyes to the moist parted curve of her mouth. His throat moved in a convulsive swallow and he looked away.

"When Peter was killed I told myself that if ever I

found you again I'd make you pay for what you did to him," he said hoarsely. "You wrecked his life, and nobody can be allowed to do that to another human being and get away with it."

She opened her lips again to deny, to exclaim in protest, and the burning blue eyes ripped through her.

"No, you listen to me. It was a mistake to let me see you wanted me, Caroline. You handed me my weapon on a plate and I intend to use it."

Caroline's body stiffened, the skin on the back of her neck prickling.

"You'll stay here in my house where I can keep my eye on you. No more men. No affairs. You're going to pay and pay in your own coin. I'll remind you from time to time what you're missing, what it is you want, and I shall enjoy watching you going round in circles, the way your husband went. I'm going to make you suffer the way Peter suffered. I'm going to watch you climbing the walls with frustration and I'm going to be as ruthless with you as you were with him."

She was trembling so violently she could barely stand. Her white face was filled with shock and horror. Tears glazed her eyes, but they did not fall. She saw his handsome dark face through them as though he swam underwater.

Nick drew a long uneven breath and pushed her away with a contemptuous smile.

"So now you know what's in store for you."

She couldn't have said a word to save her life. She could just stare fixedly, shivering.

"And don't imagine you'll get away," he added,

watching her. "Because this time you aren't getting ten yards. You'll stay and face the music."

She weakly shook her head, trying to speak, to tell him how wrong he was, how insane his suspicions of her were, how Peter had lied to him and to everyone else. But her tongue was frozen in her mouth and she couldn't utter a word.

He smiled cruelly, his eyes running over her in a leisurely dismissal.

"Poor Caroline, you look as if you've been run over by a truck. Did you think you'd got me as moonstruck as you had your husband? Sorry to disillusion you. I'm made of tougher material than Peter ever was. You don't get me with big green eyes and a sexy little body."

Helen called from the fireside, "What are you two doing out there? I hope you aren't plotting against me. Come here and listen to Kelly's idea...."

Nick looked toward the door. It was almost closed, barely open a crack, and Helen couldn't have a clue what had just happened, but Caroline knew she was not going to be able to walk in there and face her mother-in-law and her child at this moment. She felt weak and sick, and her eyes held a chill despair.

Nick turned back toward her, his eyes stripping her. "You had better go upstairs for half an hour. You're as white as a sheet." That seemed to give him some sort of bitter satisfaction. He smiled tightly at her. "I'll tell them you have a headache."

Caroline couldn't even move. She could not put one foot in front of another.

Nick pushed her roughly toward the stairs. "Go on,

before Kelly comes out and sees you. Your face is a dead giveaway.''

She stumbled away, shaking from head to foot, and walked up the stairs, clinging to the banister to keep upright. Nick stood at the foot of the stairs, watching her, then he turned and walked away. She heard his voice, casual, light: "Caroline has a headache. She's gone to lie down.''

"Oh, dear," Helen said, disturbed.

"I expect it was the train journey," Nick murmured. Then the door closed behind him and Caroline dragged herself the last few yards to her room. She shut the door and crumpled on the bed, the harsh sobs tearing her apart as she lay there, trembling like a leaf, her body wincing in a pain beyond anything she had ever known.

Her life had been smashed to pieces once before, and she had run from the ruins of it, gathering all her store of courage and endurance because she had to be strong for Kelly's sake; she had to lay one brick upon another somehow until she had rebuilt a life for them both.

Caroline was nervously aware of her own vulnerability. She was very feminine, very warmhearted, and left to herself she would always put her family before everything else. Although she had carved out a successful career for herself at the agency it had all been done through a need to provide for Kelly. Caroline herself was not ambitious. She would have swapped places with Deirdre any day. Deirdre had never quite understood that—she had often said how much she envied Caroline her chance of an exciting career—but

Deirdre had never been forced to wind herself up to facing such pressures. When she was working with a deadline in front of her, the urgency of Grey's constant demand that she come up with a brilliant idea always at the back of her mind, Caroline had often longed to walk out on it all.

She had coped with the pressures, of course, because she had to, but inside her head she had always hated it, and she had caved in now under the battering Nick had just given her.

How much more was life going to throw at her? When you have wound yourself up day after day, month after month, to facing all the tensions and problems of a job, a home, a child, without the support and love of a husband who shares your worries, there has to come a time when one more blow will knock you flat.

Lying on her bed in the dark room, Caroline shivered helplessly, her tears giving way to a numb silence.

Nick had just battered her to the floor, and she didn't have the strength at the moment to get up again.

"I can't bear it," she whispered into the silence, and felt her own loneliness and isolation walling her in.

There was no one she could talk to, confide in, ask for help. She couldn't go to Helen. Stricken though she was, Caroline couldn't ask for help from someone who was already badly mauled by life. She couldn't go to Frey, either, because he would speak to Nick, who wouldn't believe him and might say something as savagely wounding to the doctor as he had to Caroline. Frey was strong enough to take Nick's biting remarks, of course, but Caroline could not take the prospect of

Nick's speaking to Frey about her the way he had spoken just now. She shuddered, sickness at the back of her throat. No, anything was better than that. She couldn't bear anyone else to know what Nick thought of her.

"I hate him," she said aloud, but her voice had no conviction, only the ring of hopeless pain, and she knew she was lying.

She did not hate Nick. She winced, turning away from the admission that almost pushed itself over the threshold of her mind, but the unadmitted emotion oddly recharged her, giving her back a simulation of energy.

She forced herself off the bed and put on the light. In the mirror her face had the dead pallor of a corpse, her slanting green eyes blurred with tears, the lids pink and wet, her lashes flickering quickly and restlessly as she glanced at herself and away.

She washed in cold water and then brushed her untidy tangled hair, made up her face and restored herself to some faint imitation of normality.

When you have been knocked to the floor there is only one thing to do: get up again.

She had learned that during the bitter years with Peter when she had lived with fear and misery and guilt for so long that if it had not been for Kelly she would have flung herself under a bus. Now she had not only Kelly but Helen to protect and worry about, and as she checked her reflection again, relieved to see how calm she looked on the surface, she told herself she would rather have the burden of responsibility for them both than walk free and alone, anyway. She had told herself that in the past when she was alone at night, in the silent little bungalow, looking out of her bedroom window at the night sky and deeply conscious of the great echoing empty universe beyond her. It was a big, big world, and without Kelly her life would lack direction, point, any reason for continuance. Human beings are herd creatures who need each other's warmth, she thought. They are not built to live alone and they have to create for themselves a reason for life.

Kelly and Helen were her reasons now. Whatever Nick tried to do to her, she had to stay and face him because she had no choice.

She walked to the door, hoping she had forced all signs of grief and pain out of sight, and switched off the light before she went downstairs.

Nick wasn't in the room when she joined Helen and Kelly. After a quick look had told her as much, she smiled brightly, meeting Helen's concerned eyes.

"How's the head?"

"Fine now," Caroline said, going toward her.

"You look a bit pale." Helen wasn't blind. She knew that Caroline wasn't quite meeting her eyes.

"I hate train journeys."

Kelly looked up from the book she was reading. "I love them."

Caroline laughed and hoped it sounded like natural laughter. "Aren't you lucky!" She paused, still smiling. "Where's Nick?" That sounded okay; her voice didn't falter at all.

"He went out," Helen said, no shadow of awareness in her face or voice. "Hazel Skelton again, I suppose. He sees a good deal of her."

Caroline looked at the fire. The flames leaped up the soot-caked chimney, the acrid scent of wood smoke reaching her nostrils.

"It's cold tonight," Helen murmured.

"Isn't it!" Caroline was icy cold.

"Before we know where we are it will be Christmas."

Kelly grinned excitedly. "I want a new doll for Christmas with a doll's pram and—"

"You'll get what you're given," Caroline said, laughing, and got a disgusted grimace in return.

"This will be the first Christmas I've looked forward to for years," Helen murmured in a husky voice. "It will be wonderful to have a child in the house again."

Caroline watched the flames. The last Christmas she had spent in Skeldale had been a bitter one. Peter had been drunk most of the time and his violence had spilled over onto Kelly, ruining the season for the child. Frey had once told Caroline that what alcohol did was remove the restraints of the conscious mind. People who had been drinking revealed hidden feelings, hidden characteristics that they normally kept out of sight. Inhibitions were erased. They could say and do what they felt they could not say and do when they were sober. Caroline had often wondered what in Peter made it necessary for him to smash everything around him. Why, when he had been drinking, did he show signs of ferocity, uncontrollable rage?

Maybe Helen had touched on the truth when she said Peter's father might have ruined his character by being too strict with him, caning him for small childish offenses. Sober, Peter was never violent. Perhaps he had suppressed his anger with his father, his anger with himself because he knew deep down that he was weak; but when he drank he could release all the suppressed rage and turn it against those around him instead of shutting it in upon himself.

"You're not starting work straightaway, are you?" Helen asked, making Caroline jump.

"I haven't discussed that with Nick yet," she said.

"I hoped you would have time to look at houses with me," Helen told her, smiling eagerly. Her face had filled out a little in the past six weeks. She had more color and her eyes had lost the weary dullness that Caroline had noticed with such pain.

"Yes," Caroline said, jerking upright. If she could find a house quickly she could get away from Nick, escape the bitter threats he had made earlier. She was only going to be menaced like that while she was living under the same roof. "Yes, good idea," she added with enthusiasm. "We'll start looking tomorrow."

CHAPTER SEVEN

THEY FOUND A HOUSE in the center of town several days later. It was small, a terraced house with a neat pocket-handkerchief garden, but it had three bedrooms and was well within the price range they had decided upon. They had argued about that. Helen had wanted to buy the house herself, but Caroline insisted on doing so out of the money she had got from the sale of the bungalow. It had meant that they had to look for a house in her price range, but it also meant that she would be independent.

The local primary school was a short walk away, and Caroline could get a bus from the end of the road to Nick's factory each morning.

"It's ideal," she said as they stood in the garden and looked at the back of the house.

"It needs repainting," Helen suggested.

"But it is in good repair." The house was late Edwardian, built of rather ugly red brick, and it had been solidly built to last. The previous owners had had the roof retiled and the woodwork treated. Caroline had a surveyor's report that said that structurally the house was in good shape.

"I can do the decorating myself," she told Helen.

Helen began to laugh. "You are an amazing girl!"

she said. "Do you really think you could? Wouldn't it be better to have a professional do it?"

"Better, but more expensive," Caroline said dryly. "And of course I could. You can do anything if you try."

Nick was in to dinner that evening and listened as Helen excitedly told him about the house.

"Caroline is going to do the decorating herself," she added, looking amused again. Helen couldn't get over that.

Nick's black brows met. "Nonsense. She will be working too hard at the factory." He glanced at Caroline coolly. "I'll find someone to do it."

"You won't." Now that she had the hope of escaping from him she could look him in the eye, her face calm. "I did the decorating in our bungalow. I like doing it."

"We've asked the solicitors to hurry up the sale," Helen told him. "As we are paying for it without a mortgage there should be no delays. I'm very grateful for all you've done, Nick, and I promise we won't be imposing ourselves on you for much longer."

"You're doing nothing of the kind," Nick said shortly. "I'm happy to have you. There's no need to feel you have to hurry away."

Helen smiled at him warmly. "All the same. . . ."

"Caroline is going to be very busy setting up the new department," Nick said. "I don't want her distracted with domestic responsibilities at this stage. I suggest you let the solicitor proceed at his usual snail's pace. There's no rush."

"I'd prefer to move in as soon as we can," Caroline

said, and his blue eyes flashed to her face, sparks of anger in them.

Nick knew perfectly well that she would prefer to get out of his house and away from his threatening presence, but in front of Helen neither of them could be open about what their exchange of glances said in silence. Caroline's green eyes told him that she had every intention of getting away from him, and his icy sardonic stare told her in turn that if he could he would thwart her intentions.

He gave her a dry little smile. "When do you mean to start work? The office is ready."

"Oh, not right away," Helen said involuntarily, then apologized to him with a self-accusing smile. "I'm being selfish, aren't I? Of course she must start work for you soon."

"Next Monday?" Nick smiled back at Helen, then switched his eyes to Caroline as he spoke.

She drew a sharp breath, half-inclined to refuse, but in the end she nodded.

"Good," he said, getting up. "You'll be kept very busy once you have started."

They were not idle words, Caroline thought a week later as she sat in her new office concentrating on the file she was reading. Nick's company manufactured and exported a number of electrical goods of extreme sophistication and he had employed several different publicity firms in the past. Caroline was studying the work they had done and realizing that she was going to have to come up with something much better if she was to justify the existence of her department.

She lifted her head and propped it on one hand, gazing out of the window, her face abstracted.

"Don't daydream." Nick's curt voice made her start, her green eyes wide and vague as they met his across the office.

"I wasn't," she said, coloring, the vulnerable curve of her throat moving in a swallowed anger.

He was standing in the doorway, a lean tall man in a dark striped suit and a city shirt with pale red stripes, looking oddly out of place in the bustling factory. Caroline drew a shaky breath, looking away from him. In some ways he frightened her more than Peter had ever done. Peter's violence had been unpredictable, unstable, without reason and completely beyond control, but Nick Holt had reason for his rage and the antagonism in his blue eyes bit into her. Her only reaction to Peter had been a desire to stay out of his way while he was drunk. She did not want to think about how Nick made her feel.

He came into the room and glanced at the papers on her desk. "How is it coming?"

"I'm getting an idea of your products and the sort of clients you're aiming at."

He nodded. "Good. What are you doing tonight?"

"Tonight?" she repeated blankly.

"It's time you met the other directors. The Skeltons are giving a cocktail party this evening and you're invited."

She did not want to go, but as she met those hard blue eyes she knew he intended her to and wasn't going to accept a refusal.

He read her expression and threw her a mocking

smile. "Wear something pretty," he murmured. "You'll be on display. We want them to like what they see, don't we?" The mockery sharpened. "Most men do, though, don't they, when they look at you?" He put out a long finger and pushed back a soft curl of honey-blond hair from her flushed face. "Very tempting," he drawled, and then he was gone, the door closing with a snap.

She stared furiously at the closed door. Did he have to look at her, talk to her, as though she were despicable?

It is never easy to bear injustice. It isn't only children who burn with indignation and wail, "It isn't fair!" when someone wrongly accuses them. Caroline longed to prove to Nick how wrong he was about her, but she could see no way of doing so.

That evening she came downstairs in a warm brown velvet dress with a modest rounded neckline and cape-like sleeves that reached her elbows. Her hair was loose about her face, and a delicate fragrance floated around her. She had taken some trouble over her appearance. She wanted to look both attractive and efficient, as Nick hoped to impress his board of directors with her.

He was drinking by the fire, a glass of whiskey in one hand, and looked up as she came in. For a second his eyes stayed fixed on her, his face unreadable; then he looked back at his glass without a word and swallowed the remaining whiskey.

Putting down the glass, he said curtly, "Ready?"

Caroline wanted to hit him. She knew she looked good—she had made sure of that—and Nick's dismissive stare infuriated her.

She had already discovered that he was popular with both office and shop-floor workers, but perhaps he wasn't so tersely unpleasant to them. He employed large numbers of women. The electrical components he made needed deft fingers to assemble and he had told her that women were better at the job than men. As he walked around the factory with Caroline he had got quite a few covetous glances from the girls. Smiles met him everywhere he looked. *They should see him now,* she thought. With his black brows in that jagged line, his blue eyes cold and cutting, he wasn't quite so charming.

They drove along the dark moorland road slowly. Sheep grazed on these hills and at night they tended to wander along the roads, which could be dangerous to a car going at speed. Once or twice Nick had to sound his horn to frighten a sheep out of his way, and the animal would turn with startled eyes glowing in the headlights and leap away into the dark.

The Skelton house was a long modern building with white walls and gray-tiled roof, set in a grassed garden that was surrounded by moorland. It was lit from top to bottom now, the driveway full of cars parked close together, and as she got out of the car Caroline could hear voices, laughter, music.

Nick joined her and they walked up to the front door without speaking. Nick rang the bell and a girl opened the door. She was a small brunette in a low-cut red dress, her flushed face lively as she smiled at Nick.

"You're late! I ought to have you shot; I was counting on you to help me entertain them all." She had a smoky voice with a definite accent that Caroline could not place but which must be, she imagined from what Helen had told her, some sort of colonial twang. Hazel Skelton's dark brown hair was short and curled around her face. Her eyes were brown, too, but rather hard and very bright, which also went for her smile. That was hard and had a faintly acquisitive streak as she took Nick's hand in her own.

"This is Caroline Storr," he told her. "Our new publicity woman."

"Hello," Hazel said, giving her a summing-up and dismissive look. "Come in and make yourself at home." She smiled, but it was a surface smile that never reached her eyes, and when she had bestowed it on Caroline she took it away and gave it much more warmly to Nick, saying, "What have you been doing with yourself? I don't see nearly enough of you, you swine! All work and no play, remember? Do you know what I'm going to get you for Christmas? A ball and chain. That will slow you down."

Caroline followed the pair into a long crowded room, and a number of faces turned to stare at them, eyes assessing her curiously. Hazel pulled Nick's hand. "Come and say hello to daddy." She began to move away.

Nick coolly detached himself. "In a second," he said, turning to Caroline. "Caroline, come and meet Mr. Skelton." His voice made that an order delivered in the accents of authority, and when she met his eyes there was a familiar glitter in them that surprised her.

She did not like either the voice or the eyes, but as she looked up at him, prickling with indignation, someone said warmly behind her, "Caroline, this is fantastic! I didn't know you were coming; I hadn't expected to see you tonight.''

She turned, her face surprised, smiling. ''Frey! Don't tell me you've managed to get a free evening for once!''

''I've got a locum for the night,'' he admitted, smiling at her in turn. ''So I won't have to stick to one glass of sherry.'' His eyes were amused. ''Be warned,'' he added. ''After two drinks I start swinging from chandeliers.''

Laughing, Caroline admired his elegant suit. ''You're dressed to kill for the occasion, I see.'' The dark red velvet had an oddly theatrical air that did not seem quite the sort of choice she would have imagined Frey would make. He was usually so restrained in his dress, but then in this quiet country district patients expected their doctor to be very restrained and formal.

''And you are ravishing,'' he told her, sweeping his eyes over her brown velvet dress. ''We're a matching pair. We shall have to stay close together so that people can admire us.''

''Caroline's not here to enjoy herself,'' Nick cut in brusquely. ''She's working.'' Under his harsh brows the blue eyes burned with anger. He took her elbow, his fingers hurting. ''Excuse me, Forrester.''

Marched away like a recalcitrant schoolgirl, Caroline looked back at Frey. ''See you later, Frey,'' she said, smiling deliberately. Nick was not going to dictate her social life to her and he needn't think he was!

He recognized the defiance for what it was and gave her a look promising reprisals later, his fingers tightening.

Mr. Skelton shook hands vigorously. He did everything with vigor, she was to discover. He was a short broad man who bounced with energy and vim, and who found England, he told her, far too slow, far too conservative. "This town needs waking up. You'll find it quiet after London, Caroline. Nothing much for young people to do. Hazel must take you around, introduce you to some of her friends. Hazel has hundreds; she knows everyone worth knowing around here."

Caroline and Hazel looked at each other, and Hazel's lively face held no enthusiasm. She had already decided that Caroline was not worth adding to her collection of people worth knowing, and she was not about to pretend a friendliness she did not feel.

Nick introduced Caroline to several other men, all of whom were directors of his firm, she discovered. They were all much of an age and she found it hard to distinguish one from the other. They were smooth and well dressed and polite and completely unmemorable.

Listening to their conversation, she could understand why Mr. Skelton fidgeted restlessly. He had more energy than the rest of them put together.

Nick vanished with Hazel after a few moments, and Caroline edged slowly out of the group of men as they began to discuss a golfing story hole by hole by hole.

They did not even notice. She carefully made her way through the talking groups of people, meaning to sit down in a corner, but Frey spotted her and moved over to join her, smiling.

"Escaped?" he teased.

She made a face at him. "You hit the nail on the head."

"Dull lot," he agreed, keeping his voice down and grinning. "I often wonder why I go to these parties."

"Why do you?"

He shrugged. "My social life isn't exactly crammed. May I get you another drink?"

She thanked him, nodding. He slid away and came back with a glass in each hand. "Helen tells me you've bought a house on Wilverton Street."

"Yes—we were lucky to find a place so quickly." She began to tell him about the house and Frey listened, watching her, his gray eyes thoughtful. When she stopped talking he smiled at her.

"Do you like art?"

Caroline laughed. "Art? I suppose so." It was as good a subject for a party conversation as any other, she imagined.

"I paint watercolors," he said, rather flushed. "There's an exhibition of local art starting next week at the town hall—would you like to come? They are having a private viewing the night before it opens officially, and I'd be delighted if you would come with me."

"I didn't know you painted, Frey," she said, taken aback.

He grimaced. "I don't broadcast the fact. My patients would probably think it was a delinquent hobby. They have a very suspicious attitude toward art. If they found out I painted in my spare time they would start imagining that I was going to go off to live on a desert island and paint naked native girls."

"Would you like to?" she asked, teasing him.

"Maybe next year," he said, his eyes wrinkling.

"I can just see you as a beachcomber," Caroline said, laughing, her green eyes alight with amusement at the very idea. Frey was the last person in the world for such an adventure.

"Will you come to the private viewing with me?" he pressed, and she nodded.

"I'd love to, of course. I can't wait to see what sort of pictures you paint."

He grimaced. "I can tell you now—very bad ones."

"How modest," she mocked.

"There you are," grated Nick's voice beside her, and her glass tilted in her hand, liquid splashing out of it. "I had an idea I'd find you with Forrester," Nick said. "It's time we left. Are you ready to go?"

"It's early yet," Frey protested, glancing at his watch.

"Caroline has to be up early," Nick informed him through his teeth. "And it is nearly eleven. By the time we get home and she gets to bed it will be midnight. She has to be up at seven-thirty."

"So do I," Frey mourned, sighing. "I was hoping to forget."

"Sorry," Nick said untruthfully, his blue eyes antagonistic.

"Good night, Frey," Caroline said, putting down her glass.

"Don't forget," Frey said. "Next Tuesday. It starts at eight o'clock."

She nodded. "I won't forget."

"What won't you forget?" Nick asked her icily as he helped her into his car a few moments later.

She looked up, baffled. "What?"

"Forrester told you not to forget something that's going to be happening next Tuesday at eight o'clock."

He walked around and got into the driver's seat, turning to watch her with one arm along the seat.

"Oh, that," she said. "It's an art exhibition at the town hall. I promised to go with Frey."

Nick's hand tapped the seat, his long fingers drumming angrily. "I thought I told you that you weren't to see him."

"You've no jurisdiction over me," she defied him, anger in her eyes. "Who the hell do you think you are?" Caroline had a calm and level temper, but suddenly it flared out of hand, her face reddening. "Do you really imagine I'm going to let you dictate to me like that? I'm a free agent, and if I want to see Frey I will, and you won't stop me. I shall do precisely as I choose."

He eyed her, his jawline taut, then swung and started the car. It shot away into the darkness of the moors, engine racing, the miles eaten up at a speed that made her heart turn over in panic.

"Slow down! Are you trying to kill us?"

He swerved violently to avoid a sheep on the road and she clutched at his arm, trembling.

"Nick!"

He slowed down gradually, but his profile had the cutting edge of a razor, and she could feel the vibration of his anger as he drove the rest of the way home. He parked and she hurriedly got out of the car in the hope of getting into the house and up the stairs before he caught up with her. The house was dark and silent. Everyone else was in bed and Caroline felt her isolation with Nick intensely.

"Oh, no," he said harshly, grabbing her shoulder as she hurried toward the stairs. "No, you don't, Caroline. We've got some talking to do."

"I want to go to bed," she said huskily.

"You do! What do you think I want?"

The thick exclamation made her legs turn weak under her. Their eyes met and a heated excitement washed over her before she hurriedly detached her own stare, shivering.

Nick laughed sardonically under his breath, then he pulled her into the sitting room, easily controlling her angry struggles. The fire was banked for the night, smoldering softly in the darkness, and Nick switched on a table lamp and turned to look down at her flushed averted face.

"I told you—you're not to see Forrester. Do you understand me, Caroline? You're not to make dates with him!"

"What right do you think you have to order me around like this?" She lifted her head, her voice vehement.

"I don't care about rights," Nick said shortly. "I'm going to make sure you don't destroy Forrester the way you did Peter."

"It isn't true," she said huskily, shaking her head, and he watched the soft warm curls as though they fascinated him.

His hand came up and seized a handful of them, tugged to pull her head back. Caroline's green eyes stared at him with a disturbed uneasiness.

"You're beautiful," he said hoarsely. "And I want you."

Her heart stopped and started again, fierce and rapid inside her chest. Nick bent toward her, his face intent, and she met his mouth briefly, standing on tip-toe, then drew back at once, shuddering.

"No," she told him, angry with herself because for a second she had been so bitterly tempted.

"That's not what you mean, Caroline," he mocked in a husky voice. "Are we playing one of your games? What am I expected to do now—pursue you on my knees? I'm afraid that isn't my scene. I don't go in for sophisticated game playing, and if you imagine you will ever have the upper hand with me, you're very wrong. Peter might not have been able to cope with you, but I can and I intend to."

"Nick, you've got to believe me," she began in a desperate attempt to *make* him believe her, her eyes pleading with him.

His fingers played with her hair, stroked the warm curve of her cheek and followed the delicate convolutions of her ear. "Save your breath," he advised, watching her. "Just remember—you're not to start seeing Forrester. He isn't having you."

"Nick...."

"You'll regret it if you do see him."

The feel of his fingers on her skin and hair was making her increasingly weak. She looked at him, her mouth trembling, and he began breathing like a man who is on the edge of an explosion, his deep chest rising and falling rapidly.

"Don't look at me like that," he grated, his face taking on an odd pallor, a harshness that was frightening. His eyes stared down into hers, a strained glitter in his gaze. "What goes on behind those green eyes? I'm going round in circles trying to understand you, trying to make you add up. You're an enigma. Your face is so beautiful, I look at you and I wonder if I'm crazy. How can you be so many women all in one?"

Caroline listened, her face disturbed, afraid of him when he looked at her like that.

"You gave up a highly paid job to come back here and live with an old woman—"

"I love Helen," she said indignantly.

He drew a long breath. "Yes," he admitted. "And she loves you. I know. I'm not blind. I respect Helen. I'd have sworn she was too shrewd to be taken in, but she must have been. She must!"

"Must she, Nick?" Caroline kept her eyes on him.

His face tautened. "Maybe she just isn't clever enough," he muttered. "Maybe she's too innocent to imagine what goes on behind that sweet face of yours." He moved restlessly. "And Kelly...with her you're always patient, firm, loving. You're a good mother; I can't deny it."

The harsh expression on his face indicated that he wished he could find a way of denying it, and Caroline sighed.

"How does it all fit?" he demanded, catching her face between his hands and holding it tightly, staring at her. "How do I add up the equation? Sometimes I wonder if I'm going out of my mind, the way Peter did. You're tormenting me. You're under my skin like a sharp little thorn and I can't get you out."

"Doesn't it occur to you that some of the pieces don't fit because they aren't true?" Caroline asked him gently. "Can't you put some trust in your own judgment and stop believing every word Peter said to you?"

A wave of dark red swept up his face. "Oh, you'd like that, wouldn't you? Then you'd really have me where you want me."

"Nick, listen to me!"

"Peter was my cousin. He trusted me. He had to talk to someone; he poured it all out to me every time I saw him. He talked of nothing else but you—his jealousy, the men you were seeing, how you had betrayed him with people he trusted, like Forrester." He broke off, his jawline harsh. "He never suspected me. I was the last person in the world he would have dreamed...." His voice stopped on a deep wrenched note and Caroline looked at him sharply, her brows meeting, her face distressed.

I must have been blind, she thought with a sense of shock and understanding and compassion for him. *Why didn't I realize how he felt before?*

"I've lived with it ever since," he said thickly. "I despised Peter because he couldn't hold you although you were his wife, because he let you drive him crazy. Now you're trying to drive me crazy."

"I'm not trying to do anything to you, Nick. If you really believe that, all you have to do is give me a wide berth, stay away from me—"

"I can't," he said deeply. "When I came looking for you in London I told myself I was going to treat you with the contempt you deserved. I was going to make it very clear I detested you."

"You made it clear."

He shook his head, staring down at her. "If I could only be sure," he muttered. "You're like a dissolving image on film. You seem to change all the time inside my head, fade from one face to another, and I can never make up my mind which is the real you. I can't stop watching you to find out. I have to know. I'm confused, bewildered, and I'm really beginning to understand what happened to Peter now. He must have gone through this, too." He drew a long hard breath. "But you aren't driving me insane—not me, Caroline. I'm going to do what Peter should have done—I'm going to lock you up and throw away the key. Maybe then he'll stop haunting me," he added, his voice shaking.

"Haunting you?" she asked, staring at him, her face pale.

Bitterness filled his face. "He doesn't haunt you? You sleep easily at night, do you? You don't suffer from guilt or self-reproach, I suppose. It doesn't bother you at all to remember what you did to him?"

The suspicion that had been growing inside her in the past few minutes became a hard certainty, and Caroline said involuntarily, "It's you who feels guilty, isn't it?"

He looked at her in shock, his face white now, and the blue eyes were almost black with pain. There was a long silence, then he said heavily, "Oh, yes, I feel guilty. How do you expect me to feel? What do you think it cost me to listen to him when all the time I was hating him because you were his wife and I wanted you like hell myself?"

Caroline wished she could think of something to say

to him that might relieve the self-inflicted wounds she could see now in his face. Nick's anger was not all turned in her direction; a lot of it was channeled toward himself. It is much easier to hate someone else than to hate yourself. It is much easier to blame someone else than to blame yourself. Nick loathed himself because he had wanted his cousin's wife. He blamed himself because Peter had gone to pieces and got killed. He had not consciously made her the scapegoat for what he had felt himself, but his self-loathing had deepened his anger and contempt for her.

He seemed to find her level gaze unbearable. Swinging away, he slammed out of the room, and she heard him going out of the house, the front door crashing behind him.

CHAPTER EIGHT

FREY RANG HER on the Tuesday morning. She was working on her ideas for a campaign to be launched in Australia some months ahead, and when the phone rang she detached her mind with difficulty.

"Oh, hello, Frey," she said absently, then sat up. "Frey? Is something wrong? Helen?"

"Nothing's wrong," he said quickly, a smile in his voice. "You're too uptight, Caroline. Calm down. This is pleasure, not business."

"That's nice," she said, smiling, too.

"I just wanted to remind you about tonight."

Caroline bit her lip, frowning. There was a moment of hesitation, and Frey said quickly, "Don't say you can't come; I shall be very disappointed."

Caroline looked at the door. Why should she turn down invitations to an innocuous art exhibition merely to placate a man who hated her?

"Of course I'm coming," she said warmly and with determination.

"Fantastic," Frey said, his voice lightening. "Look, could we have a meal first? It would have to be a quickie and there isn't much choice around here, but we could have chicken in a basket at the pub opposite the town hall."

Caroline was amused. "Sounds great, thank you."

"Pick you up at six-thirty?" Frey asked after Helen and Kelly and then rang off, and Caroline went back to her ideas session without being able to keep her mind on the job this time. She had no doubt that when Nick found out she had defied him there would be a row, but apart from shouting at her, making nasty remarks and nastier threats, what could he do? She was not his property and he had no right to dictate her private life. Let him snarl.

She ate in the canteen every day; the food was very cheap and it saved time even if it wasn't cordon-bleu cooking. As she came back from lunch that day she saw Nick's car shoot away from the factory. He was not alone in it: Hazel Skelton sat beside him. She was wearing a silver gray fox jacket and a tiny black hat with an even tinier veil. She looked sophisticated and very pretty, and Caroline hoped they would enjoy their lunch, or whatever they were planning to do. They wouldn't be eating in the canteen, she knew.

That evening she mentioned having seen Hazel with Nick to Helen, who grimaced.

"Eat in the canteen? Hazel Skelton? You've got to be joking! The girl's an appalling snob."

"Nick seems to like her," Caroline said casually.

"Oh, well," Helen muttered, her face wry. "Men— what do they ever know about women? You've seen her with him. Sweet as honey whenever he's around."

"She does seem to be more of a man's woman."

"She's a—" Helen cut the word off, chuckling. "I won't say it. My husband would have had fifty fits if he had ever heard me use a word like that."

"Word like what?" Caroline met her eyes, her mouth twitching.

"Don't give me that innocent look," Helen teased. "Of course you'd never dream of swearing, would you?"

"Me? Never," Caroline said, and they both laughed.

When Caroline told her that she was going out for the evening with Frey, Helen looked almost girlish with excitement, her face flushed.

"What are you going to wear? I like you in that brown velvet. Frey does, too. He mentioned it last time he called, and that's a sure sign. Men don't often remember what a woman was wearing, so it must have made quite an impression on him."

Caroline eyed her thoughtfully and with wary curiosity. Was she imagining things or was Helen matchmaking for her? Helen was deeply fond of Frey. He was her ideal man and she felt she owed him a great deal. Caroline hoped Helen hadn't got the wrong idea. Nice though Frey was, Caroline knew she could never feel any more than friendship for him. She enjoyed his company, she liked him, and that was it.

"You will wear the brown velvet, won't you?" Helen pressed, and Caroline agreed that she would, more because she did not have a very wide choice than because she wanted to please Frey. She tended to buy clothes that would last, avoiding the instant fashion that can date within months, because ever since she'd left Skeldale she'd had to be careful with money and she couldn't afford to buy anything on impulse.

As she was dressing, she thought about Helen's

determined efforts to interest her in Frey. Even when people think they are acting in someone else's interest they are often prompted by motives of their own. No doubt Helen had thought up excellent reasons why Caroline and Frey would be a perfect pair, but her desire to push them together had her own fondness and admiration for Frey as a trigger.

That applied to Nick, too. His contempt and anger toward her sprang from his own contempt and anger with himself for the way he had felt about her. He felt guilty about Peter and thought she should feel guilty, too. Nick felt her guilt was worse than his. He believed Peter's lies—he thought she had betrayed Peter over and over again—and quite apart from despising her for that, he instinctively picked up from her an absence of guilt. That made him bitterly angry with her.

Nick's feelings indicated just what he thought of her, how he saw her, and she burned with indignation at his picture of her character.

All human beings are a tangled web of contradictions and confusions. Caroline loved Helen and she knew that Helen would never do anything that might hurt her. Helen had stood by Peter without flinching throughout the last terrible years. She had never complained and she had never blamed her son. Helen was a wonderful woman and Caroline had nothing but admiration for her, yet all the same, Helen was a contradictory human being, too, and she was capable of the emotional sleight of hand that could confuse her honest desire to see Caroline happy with her equally honest desire to repay some of the debt she felt she owed to Frey.

It is easier to imagine we see others clearly than to face up to ourselves. Looking at herself in the mirror, Caroline shied away from so much as the attempt. She did not want to know what was going on inside her own head. She preferred to ignore the danger signals she got whenever she saw Nick. All she would get from him was pain, and she had had enough pain. She had been like someone struggling in turbulent waters to save her life for years, and all she wanted now was a little peace and quiet, an interlude in which she could let her tired mind and strained nerves relax.

"Are you going out, mummy?" Kelly demanded when she went downstairs.

Caroline nodded, smiling.

"Where?"

"With Dr. Forrester."

Kelly's face dropped. "Not Uncle Nick?"

Her mother eyed her dryly. Not another one with her own ax to grind and her own tangled web of motivations!

"Not Uncle Nick," she agreed shortly.

"You like Uncle Nick, don't you, mummy?" Kelly couldn't believe there was a living soul who did not adore her hero. Nick had treated her with indulgent kindness from the day he arrived at their bungalow to take them away, and Kelly thought the sun shone out of him. Nick was tall and handsome and had a fantastic car, and he seemed to know precisely how to talk to a little girl of seven. Caroline had watched them together. Nick made Kelly feel special. When Frey talked to her, there was always the faintest, almost undetectable tinge of patronage in his voice. Frey never forgot Kelly was a little girl. Nick managed to make it seem that he did. He treated Kelly as though she were a princess and she loved it.

Clever, Caroline thought bitterly. *He's clever. With little girls and girls like Hazel Skelton he is spectacularly successful, but he doesn't waste any of his charm on me.*

Kelly was gazing at her in disbelief, her mouth open. "Don't you, mummy? Don't you love Uncle Nick? I do, I love Uncle Nick, and you're mean." She punched her mother crossly and ran out, scowling.

"Oh, dear," Helen said, laughing and completely unaware. "She's upset now."

"She'll get over it," Caroline said curtly, hoping her face had not flushed too revealingly, but Helen had no eyes for her at that moment because Frey had arrived and she was beaming at him approvingly.

"Don't you look smart! Doesn't he look smart, Caroline?"

Frey met Caroline's eyes, his expression rueful. "Don't answer that."

"You've got your Gauguin outfit on again," she teased, and Helen stared at her blankly.

"What, dear? His what?"

"Never mind," Frey said, laughing. "Don't ask. She's pulling my leg."

Helen liked that. It made them sound intimate, people who had secrets and private jokes, and she approved of that. Her eyes were very bright as she saw them off, and Caroline sighed. She hoped Frey wasn't picking up Helen's not-so-hidden thoughts. That could be very awkward.

Frey was oddly nervous, she noted. He was talking rather faster than he usually did and the calm tone of his mind was not visible this evening. Caroline was bothered by that. Was Frey embarrassed by Helen's obvious excitement about their going out together? Even worse, was Frey more interested in her than she had thought? She did not want to hurt him, but she knew she could never think of him as anything more than a friend. It would be painful to have to let him see that.

They had fried chicken and salad in a large busy pub in the High Street, and talked about Frey's partner, Skeldale and mutual acquaintances.

"What made you take up painting?" she asked when he paused in his string of slightly husky remarks.

Frey made a face at her. "God knows. At this moment I wish I'd never touched a brush."

Caroline's green eyes widened and she gazed at him with the beginning of a smile. So that was what was eating him! Not her at all! *How easy it is to misunderstand,* she thought. She had been acutely uneasy about Helen's desire to matchmake, but Frey hadn't been thinking about either her or Helen. Frey had been thinking about Frey, and that was the human condition: that was all people ever thought about—themselves. She looked into Frey's normally calm face and liked him even more because he was human; he wasn't entirely the saint Helen thought him. Frey was a devoted, tireless doctor who gave of himself freely to his patients, but he was also a human being and tonight he was very nervous because he had exposed himself by putting some of his paintings into this exhibition.

"You still haven't told me what sort of pictures you paint," she pointed out.

"Watercolors," he said.

"Landscapes?"

He nodded, fiddling with his glass of white wine.

"Local places?"

It was like getting blood out of a stone. He didn't want to talk about his painting. It was obsessing him, though, she saw. He kept looking at his watch, and there was a little tic beside his mouth. Frey was nervous.

The exhibition was in a bare hall, people's feet creaking on the wooden floorboards as they tiptoed around from canvas to canvas in a reverent way, their voices hushed.

Caroline and Frey moved around, too, glasses of sherry in their hands. Frey was smiling, but it was a forced smile. Looking at some of the gaudy oil paintings of Yorkshire landscapes, Caroline couldn't see that he had much to worry about. He couldn't be much worse than those.

There were not many watercolors, and as soon as Caroline spotted one she looked in her catalog—run off by hand on the local school machine, Frey had told her—and saw that it was one of Frey's pictures.

He fidgeted beside her, clearing his throat. His ears were red. Caroline looked at the stormy landscape, the greens and grays delicately fading into each other, the detail picked out with clarity and precision.

"Frey, it's good," she said spontaneously, turning to look at him. "It's really good, the best we've seen; you must know it is! I'm impressed."

His face brightened slightly, but only slightly, and he looked at the picture and made a face. "I didn't get that sky right. I took days over it, but it just wouldn't come the way I wanted it. Every time I see the damned thing my fingers itch. I'd like to do it again. It makes me feel irritated just to see it. When you've got a picture in your head and then it comes out all wrong, it drives you mad."

"It must," she said, surprised by his passionate outburst. They walked on and there were two other pictures. Neither of them was quite as good as the first, but Frey seemed less bothered by them. It was the first painting that he went back to and looked at with a ferocious scowl.

"That's your favorite, isn't it?" Caroline asked, smiling.

"I can't stand the sight of it," he said, walking away, and she followed him with amusement. He introduced her to other artists who were exhibiting and they stayed talking for a couple of hours. They each had another glass of sherry, but Frey did not need alcohol anyway. He was wound up, excited, his calm entirely dissolved, and Caroline watched him with curiosity as he talked and argued and praised the work of his friends. Who would have thought that behind Frey's quiet manner lurked this colorful streak? The red velvet dinner jacket, the painting, the nervous excitement—these suggested a side of Frey his patients never saw. But who says that people have to be one-dimensional, flat, always predictable?

Frey hummed under his breath as he drove her home. "I hope you weren't bored, Caroline."

"Not a bit; I enjoyed myself enormously."

"Did you?" He smiled at her, very pleased. "Have you ever thought of taking up a hobby?"

"When would I find the time?" Her eyes danced, and he smiled at her, but seriously.

"I agree, it isn't easy, but you've no idea what a difference it can make. It gives you a new angle on life. I've only one regret about taking up painting—I didn't start soon enough. I wish I'd started years ago."

Caroline watched his flushed excited face. "Do you think you might have taken it up as a profession if you'd started when you were at school?"

His face shifted, hesitation and uncertainty in his gray eyes. "I don't know," he said at last, and she noted that he did not say that he had never considered the idea. She got the feeling Frey had wondered that himself.

"But I didn't," he said flatly. "And I love medicine. I love working with people. I know it's unfashionable to say so, but I like people and I want to help them." He grimaced self-derisively at her, shrugging. "That sounds like do-goodism, I know. I'm always hearing it said that if you claim you want to help other people you're just being self-indulgent and it's yourself you want to help; you're only doing the job because of what's in it for you. They may be right, the people who say that, but I'm no good at self-analysis and I've got a simple mind. I just know I'm happiest when I'm taking care of sick people. They need me, and if I'm getting something out of it for myself without realizing it, that doesn't seem to me to matter. All this social pyschology sounds intriguing, but when you get down to it all that matters is that someone who's sick needs help and isn't going to ask whether the doctor's taking out his appendix because he gets a kick out of saving lives or because he's Albert Schweitzer."

He had paused, apparently because he had run out of breath, and Caroline smiled at him.

"I couldn't agree more."

"Thank you," he said wryly. "I'm glad about that."

They both laughed, and Frey said, "Sorry to get onto my soapbox like that."

"No need to apologize. You were just talking common sense."

"That's another unfashionable commodity," he murmured. The car turned into the drive and pulled up outside Nick's house. Frey turned and looked at her with a smile in his gray eyes.

"You know, you're very easy to talk to. You listen beautifully."

Caroline began to laugh. "How does one do that?"

"By making it easy for the person doing all the talking to feel he's got your full attention," he said. "Thank you. Thank you for coming along this evening, too. I enjoyed myself more than I can tell you."

"So did I," Caroline told him. "And I thought your favorite painting was pretty impressive, whether you got the sky exactly how you wanted it or not."

"I like you, Caroline Storr," Frey said, laughing. "You can criticize my paintings anytime you like."

The house was dark when she let herself in, but through the closed door of the sitting room she saw a faint crack of light and heard Hazel Skelton's smoky voice murmuring in seductive undertones.

Caroline went upstairs, her face stiff. Hazel Skelton was welcome to Nick! Was he fondling her the way he fondled the dogs, his long fingers softly moving in her scented hair? In her bedroom Caroline looked into the mirror and saw very bright, very angry green eyes and looked away again.

NEXT MORNING she was busy at her desk when Nick strode into the office, his temper racing like an engine at full throttle, the blue eyes discharging a trail of angry blue sparks at her.

"You went, I gather."

She looked at him with defiance, her chin raised.

"What are you talking about?"

"You know very well what I'm talking about!" He came over to her and bent toward her, talking with almost closed lips. "Don't think you're going to get away with it. You aren't. I gave you fair warning. You can take the consequences."

He was gone again before she could think of anything to say, the door crashing after him.

She was nervous for the rest of the day, and that was absurd, because what could he do to her? It had just been an empty threat, she told herself, yet all the same, Nick's furious blue eyes had left her uneasy.

She heard the next day that the firm had been offered a large contract by an Arab country that needed some electrical hardware urgently. The whole place swung into frenzied activity and Nick was kept very busy making sure the delivery date was met. Caroline was relieved to find that for the moment he had no time to remember the threat he had made to her. He rarely arrived home until late at night and in the factory he was too preoccupied with work to do more than spare a brief glance for her when he saw her.

Winter deepened around them, the wind tipped with ice and the sky a dull leaden gray. Helen was concerned about Nick's long working hours and kept urging Caroline to persuade him to cut them down. "If you get a chance to talk to him at work today, make him see how silly he's being," she said anxiously. "He works far too hard."

He did, Caroline agreed. His striding figure moved around the factory all day, keeping things moving, watching every part of the manufacturing process. He was liked by the people who worked for him; Caroline had soon realized that. He had their respect, their admiration, their trust, and it was not an easy matter to gain the admiration of the people of Skeldale. They were sturdy-minded, shrewd, reluctant to commit themselves to anyone until he had proved himself. Nick's character would have to be a powerful one to impress the people of Skeldale.

It was common gossip that Hazel Skelton was very impressed. Bets were laid on whether or not Hazel was going to persuade him to marry her. Largely the men approved of her, the women did not. The men thought her sexy, very pretty. "Aye, she's a fancy bird; I wouldn't mind her myself," one of the engineers said, grinning widely.

The women took a different view. "He must be going soft in the head, dating that one. Anyone with half an eye can see what she's like, and he's such a lovely fella.'' The two typists at the next table had spent their whole lunch break talking about Nick and Hazel Skelton, and Caroline had tried to turn a deaf ear but for some unaccountable reason found herself picking up every word that was said about Nick, even across the canteen at its most crowded.

She crossly shook ginger all over her slice of melon and then couldn't eat it because it made her feel sick. Her mood was sharp lately. Pressure at work, she assured herself; that was what it was. It had nothing whatever to do with Nick Holt. He hated her on extremely unfair grounds and Caroline was angry with him. She didn't care what he thought. If he wanted to date Hazel Skelton, good luck. It would serve him right if Hazel married him, which Caroline felt would be a fate far worse than death for any sane man, and she would be only too delighted to chuck confetti at the pair of them. She would even resist the temptation to chuck a few stones, as well.

That evening Helen had a headache and went to bed soon after Kelly had gone upstairs. Caroline ate dinner alone. She was restless and irritable and couldn't sit still in the cozy sitting room by the roaring fire. She felt she had to get out, walk, do something to stop the little wheels of her mind going round in ever decreasing circles.

Putting on an old fur-lined anorak, she stepped into her Wellingtons and went out. It was a chilly winter night, the wind whistling over the moors and making the bare trees lash violently backward and forward against the stormy sky, the creak of their branches eerie. The moon moved softly between wind-driven clouds, lending a livid light to the outline of the rolling hills in the far distance.

Caroline had to make her way carefully. The ground was soft and swampy in places. In others, rough tussocks of heather rose in her path, scratching at her boots as she made her way through them.

She wouldn't let herself think. She didn't dare. The minute she let down her guard, Nick sprang into her mind like the demon king in a pantomime, and tonight she needed to escape him, not take him with her everywhere she went.

Pausing, she looked back at the house. It loomed among the trees, black and solid, one lighted window the only sign of life in it.

I mustn't go too far, she thought. It was easy to get lost out there, especially at night when all the landmarks were obscured. A car engine throbbed in the silence and a beam of yellow light cut across the moors toward her before it vanished behind the house.

Nick was home, she thought, and turned and plunged forward into the dark. She certainly was not going back there while he was up. She would wait until she could be sure he had gone to bed. The house was never locked, even at night. Out here on the cold moors there was little risk of being visited by burglars, and people in Skeldale largely knew each other, trusted each other.

Stumbling along, she kept her eyes on the moon as it silently passed between one bank of cloud and another, the silvery light revealing the moorland for a moment before it vanished and cloaked the rough terrain in darkness again.

Nick had asked her what sort of woman she was; he had bitterly said he couldn't make her add up, could not understand her at all. But Caroline might well have asked him the same question. What sort of man could live under the same roof with her for weeks and still refuse to admit any doubts about the lies Peter had told him? Caroline resented that.

Most people have a picture of themselves inside their heads, an image they have somehow formed through the years when they were growing up, and that image is the one they imagine they project to those around them. Caroline knew what she liked. She knew she liked music and cooking and going for walks across the moor. She knew she had a deep instinct for security. She wanted to have and to give to Kelly a safe, happy home life. Ambition is for those who need it. Caroline had very little need for it. She wanted to be happy, that was basically all she wanted, and at times she wondered why her one real need should have been denied to her for most of her adult life. Life was unfair, she thought, walking faster in her frustrated anger. Why was life so muddled, so unjust and unequal?

Why couldn't she fall in love with Frey, for instance? He was a nice man, a good man, an intelligent man who would make somebody a marvelous husband if she were prepared to share him with the rest of the district and put up with his appallingly long working hours, his passion for painting, his constantly interrupted private life.

Frey would make a secure home life for any woman. He wouldn't suspect her, attack her, look at her with contempt over nothing.

Why did she have to fall in love with Nick Holt?

She stopped dead, her face stricken. *I'm not,* she thought rapidly. *I'm not in love with him. Not in love. I fancy him, maybe. I can't stop thinking about him, admittedly. But I'm not in love.*

I'd have to be crazy. I'd need my head examined. Little men in white coats should come and take me away.

She put her hands over her eyes, trembling. The wind rushed over the moors, wailing like a savage spirit, and her hair tossed in it, obscuring her face.

She wanted to run from the admission she had only just allowed to rise inside her brain, but Caroline had a strange sort of nervous courage. It had helped her to face her husband at his most violent and it had helped her to make the decision to leave him for Kelly's sake. It had helped her to work and plan and survive the years alone when she'd borne all the responsibility for her child. It was a reluctant bravery. Caroline would much have preferred to duck out of all those situations, but she had always forced herself to face things, and now she forced herself to face her feeling for Nick.

Her unconscious had known all along. During the years in London she had not forgotten Nick, and the night he forced his way into her home she had felt the shock of a stupid excitement even though she was so afraid.

You can never hide anything from yourself for long, she thought, letting her hands drop and squaring her shoulders. Sooner or later the truth bubbles up through the confused waters of the mind and bursts upon you before you can avoid it.

She couldn't stand there all night in the teeth of the wind, bewailing her luck in falling for a man who hated her. Face set, she began to march back toward the house, hoping she was going in the right direction. She couldn't see the lighted window anymore. Maybe Nick had switched that light out and gone to bed. The moon was swimming behind clouds again and Caroline peered into the pervading blackness, frowning. Which way?

She was very cold. The anorak was no longer keeping out the wind. Shivering, she began to run.

Her feet suddenly went from under her. She was falling helplessly, a muffled scream bursting out of her. It happened too fast for her to realize what had happened. She hit the rough rocky sides of a sharply sloping gully, her body crashing down and down, thudding and rolling until she reached the bottom and lay still.

CHAPTER NINE

THE NEXT THING SHE KNEW was when she heard a voice. It was talking quickly and breathlessly with a little sob in it. "It isn't fair, it isn't fair...."

Caroline's brows twitched. Who on earth...? She came back from a long way, as though she had been asleep for ages, and stirred, shivering. Her nose was pressing into something rough and wiry that scratched her soft skin.

Why am I lying on my face and what on earth am I lying on, she asked silently, turning her cheek and looking into pitch blackness.

She was cold and stiff and she hurt all over the place. Who had been talking just now?

A strangled moan broke from her chill lips as she remembered. She had fallen, fallen a long way, and she had hurt herself. She must have been knocked unconscious, and as she tried to move, and winced and bit her lip, she wished she had stayed unconscious, because her whole body was screwed up in pain.

She was going to have to get up. She breathed carefully, getting ready to drag herself to her feet, but when she made the effort the pain sent her facedown again, sobbing weakly.

She had broken her ankle. There were other injuries,

but she was not yet ready to find out what those were. When her tears had subsided she lay quietly, her hand making tentative forays over her body to try to decide just what she had done. Her ribs hurt. Every breath seemed to tear at her. She had a bruised and bleeding face. Her nose throbbed, but it didn't seem to be broken. There were scratches and grazes on her hands.

I must look a pretty sight, she thought grimly, *and I'm going to have to get back up the sides of this gully. I can't lie here until morning. It is bitterly cold and I'll die of exposure out here.*

She could not stand on her broken ankle, but she thought she could crawl if she was careful.

Her drawn breath hurt as she forced herself to start moving. Clawing at the rough ground, she began to drag herself up the sides of the gully inch by painful inch, her injured foot dangling behind her while the other took the strain of maintaining a toehold.

She had no idea how long it took. She had to keep resting, breathing carefully, and pain became a monotonous companion on the journey upward.

The last few feet were the worst. Those over, she collapsed on the flat ground at the top, shivering and crying.

She did not have the energy to move again for a while; then she felt the first heavy drop of rain on the back of her outflung hand. She twisted her neck to look up, and a few more drops splashed wetly on her face.

That was all I needed, she thought. *Rain. Lovely, just my luck. Now I shall get soaked to the skin, and on my past record I am probably about to be blessed with pneumonia.*

Well, rain or no rain, she had to get back to the house, because the only alternative was to lie there until morning when someone came looking for her, and by then she would probably be in very rough shape.

She began to crawl again. The rain became heavier and soaked into the ground around her, saturating her hair, her body, making the ground so slippery she kept sliding back instead of going forward, and she was covered in mud, her hands and face filthy, her clothes grimy.

The worst part was that she wasn't even sure she was going in the right direction, so she made herself clamber to her knees to peer through the darkness in the hope of seeing the house.

That was when she passed out for the second time, but when she opened her eyes again someone was kneeling beside her, a flashlight focused on her face. She could hear the little voice again inside her head: "Why? Why?"

"You're safe, Caroline; don't cry. For God's sake don't cry like that!"

She blinked dazedly in the brightness. "Nick?"

"I've got you; you're going to be okay." His voice was deep and husky and she couldn't see his face behind the flashlight.

She tried to squint through it, pierce the yellow brilliance to find him.

"I'm probably going to have pneumonia," she said conversationally, her white mouth quivering into a rueful smile. "Aren't I lucky?"

"Stop talking," he said brusquely.

"Sorry."

"And don't keep apologizing!"

"Was I? Sorry." She didn't remember apologizing before. His hands were touching her and she tried weakly to brush them away.

"Don't."

"I have to know where you've hurt yourself."

"Everywhere."

Nick drew an uneven breath. "What sort of pain is it?"

"The hurting kind," she said through a hammering agony in her head. *I hope I'm not going to be sick,* she thought. *Nick wouldn't like that. I must not be sick.* She peered through the light and his face was going round and round like something in a washing machine, and it was very pale, the blue eyes sharply brilliant against the whiteness of his skin.

"You look funny," said Caroline.

Nick swore.

"That's not very nice," she said in a childish voice, frowning. That was a mistake. It hurt her head. She closed her eyes. Nick was too much. She felt too ill to think about Nick at the moment.

The next hour was a nightmare. Nick picked her up in his arms and began to carry her over the moorland, her head on his shoulder and her body cradled against him out of the cutting edge of the wind. It could have been very comfortable. It could have been heaven—if she hadn't been almost crazy with pain. Every movement, every breath, hurt. Caroline kept passing out and coming back again with a strangled moan.

"Caroline, be quiet," he said once, his voice hoarse.

"Sorry."

He swore again and she said, "Sorry, didn't mean to say 'sorry.'" And laughed before she faded again into merciful oblivion, only to come back and find herself still cold, still in pain, still in Nick's strong arms out on the windy moors.

He must have been deeply relieved to put her down when he had struggled with her through the door into the sitting room. The fire had sunk to a smoldering glow that looked at her like a little morose red eye before Nick switched on the lights and she closed her eyelids to shut out that attacking brilliance.

She heard Nick dialing, heard his voice speak quickly, harshly. Her body was convulsively in the grip of pain and she shuddered from head to foot. She couldn't stop shivering. "So cold, so cold," she said mournfully.

Nick was covering her with blankets, heaping them over her with gentle hands. Her teeth chattered and the little voice came through them, "Sorry, sorry."

"Oh, for God's sake!" Nick grated. He was fed up with her, furious with her, and the tears trickled down her face as she tried to stop herself from talking. She half knew it was her, half rambled in delirium, the disjointed husky words leaking from her without her being able to stop them.

Someone softly wiped the tears away. Someone bent over her, stroking back the wet tangled hair from her face. Her teeth had stopped chattering, but she was still restless in pain, swathed from her chin to her feet in blankets.

"Nick..." she groaned.

He said, "Yes, Caroline," at her ear, his voice still

harsh with some sort of feeling—but was it anger or pain? Had he hurt himself? He sounded so odd.

Once she opened her eyes, and there were men in white coats. *They're coming to take me away,* she thought, a stifled laughter in her throat.

"Easy now," one of them said, coming and going in her field of vision.

"Just fold the blanket back," someone said. "We'll have to have that anorak off."

Caroline cried out as they lifted her with careful gentleness, and someone said, "Can't you be careful?"

"Nick . . ." she moaned. He was still angry. His voice sounded curt and terse and almost bitter.

She wanted to see him, so she forced her eyes open and looked into Frey's worried face.

"Hello, Frey," she said quite lucidly. "When did you get here?"

He gave her a little smile. "How do you feel, Caroline?"

"Terrible," she said. Her mouth moved and Frey watched, his gray eyes concerned.

"This won't hurt," he said, a hypodermic in his hand.

"Do you want to bet?" Caroline hated injections.

"There," Frey said, straightening. "Very soon nothing will hurt, I promise."

"Dear Frey," she said as she shut her eyes on a sigh and the pain began floating away from her, leaving her so tired that she lay there limply as she was taken out to the ambulance, almost blissful with the removal at last of all the grinding agony of her broken bones.

THE NEXT TIME she opened her eyes she was in a narrow white bed in a quiet ward, and gray daylight was filtering through the room like silent dust while a young nurse in a green-striped dress watched it as though she would like to get a dustpan and sweep it all up.

Caroline experimentally moved to see if anything hurt, and it did—but not as badly as it had.

"Oh, back with us, are you?" the nurse said, coming to her side and giving her a professional smile.

"Afraid so," Caroline whispered. She felt impelled to whisper. Everyone else in the long ward seemed to be asleep despite the daylight.

"What—" Caroline began to ask as the nurse coolly thrust a thermometer into her mouth. Silenced, she watched the girl pick up one of her hands and start monitoring her pulse, one eye on the watch pinned to her apron.

When the thermometer had been removed, Caroline tried again. "What's wrong with me?"

She got another professional look. "Don't you remember?"

"I remember falling down a gully on the moors," Caroline said, half smiling. Did the nurse think she was half-witted? "I meant, how badly did I hurt myself?"

"Not badly," the girl said. "You broke your ankle, busted a couple of ribs and got some bad bruises here and there, but by and large you came off quite lightly apart from the exposure."

Caroline absorbed that. "Did I sleep all night?"

She got a long stare that time. "You've been here

two days,'' the nurse informed her. "Don't you remember yesterday? I admitted you, and when I went
off yesterday morning you seemed to recognize me.''

"Did I? I don't remember a thing.''

"You were under sedation.''

"Oh,'' Caroline said, closing her eyes.

The nurse began to move away, her apron crackling.
Caroline opened her eyes. "I suppose I couldn't have a
cup of tea?''

Smiling, the girl said, "Of course you can. Sugar?''

"Yes, please.''

She lay listening to the noises the other patients
made, their breathing, faint snores, movements. A
clock ticked heavily somewhere and she heard the rat-
tle of a trolley. Then suddenly the trolley crashed
through the doors like the arrival of an express train at
Paddington Station, the ward lights blazed and the patients groaned and protested and pulled the bedclothes
over their heads.

Caroline focused on a large clock on the wall above
the main doors. Six o'clock? Six o'clock?

Frey came in that afternoon, and she said to him
teasingly, "What sort of hours do you keep in these
places? Do you know they woke me up at six?''

"Ghastly, isn't it?'' Frey smiled, his calm face
amused.

"Admit it—they run this place for their conveni-
ence, not the welfare of the patients.''

"Routine has to be followed,'' he agreed. "The
night staff have a lot to do before they can go off duty,
and that means the patients have to be kept to a strict
timetable.''

Caroline took his hand, looking at him shyly. "Thank you for coming out in the middle of the night for me. I'm sorry to have been such a nuisance to you all."

"So I should think," Frey scolded, smiling. "What on earth made you go for a ramble on the moors at that hour of the night?"

"I can scarcely remember. I must have been crazy."

"Well, you said it," he murmured, watching her. "Only an idiot would have done it."

"Sorry," she said. "Frey, will they let Kelly come and see me?"

"If you're very good and start getting better," Frey promised.

"I'm fine now."

"I don't want any argument from you," Frey told her jokingly. "Get better. That's an order. Then I'll see if Kelly can come."

Helen came that evening and sat by the bed looking at her with oddly uneasy eyes. Caroline couldn't put a finger on what was wrong, but something was: Helen wasn't quite meeting her gaze.

"How do you feel, dear? Are they looking after you?"

"Devotedly," Caroline said, watching her. "What about you? I'm sorry to have given you such a shock."

Helen sighed. "It *was* a shock. I woke up, hearing voices and banging about, and when I got downstairs there was an ambulance outside and you going out of the door on a stretcher looking half-dead."

"You should have seen me earlier," Caroline said jokingly.

Helen wasn't amused. "Oh, Caroline," she said, and tears came into her eyes. She brushed her hand over them, looking away, and Caroline was horrified.

"Helen, I'm sorry—you mustn't cry. I'm fine now, really. I'm going to be out of here in no time."

"You stay where you are," Helen said in a scolding voice. "You don't know what you look like."

"Oh," said Caroline ruefully. "Is it that bad?" She hadn't seen herself yet. She had asked for a mirror, but the nurse had not had one on hand, or so she had said, and Caroline had had to content herself with guessing that she looked pretty terrible. They had washed her and brushed her hair and let her wear the pretty pink woolly bed jacket Helen had brought in for her, but she knew her face was covered in scratches, bruises and grazes, and under her hospital-issue nightie, which appeared to be made out of a well-washed old flour sack, she had a cocoon of bandages and plasters festooned around her. Although she had been given painkillers, her ribs hurt when she breathed and her ankle hurt all the time.

She had already asked about Kelly. That had been her first question, and Helen had assured her that Kelly was fine, but Caroline couldn't stop worrying. "You're sure she's okay? She used to walk in her sleep when she was worried. . . ."

Helen frowned. "Don't worry. If I didn't hear her, Nick or Mrs. Bentall would."

"How is Nick?" Caroline inquired casually, looking away.

"Busy," Helen said in a flat voice, and changed the subject. Caroline couldn't help wondering why the subject of Nick should so obviously make Helen uneasy. Was he very angry with her? He had been angry the night he found her out on the moors, she remembered all too vividly. Was he furious even now?

The bell sounded and Helen stood up slowly. "I'll come again tomorrow," she promised.

"It will be tiring for you," Caroline protested. "Not that I don't love seeing you, but I don't want you making that journey into town every day."

"Nick drives me," Helen said, then stopped and flushed and added quickly, "Anything you want?"

"No," Caroline said. "Thank you."

Helen kissed her on her grazed cheek and walked away, and Caroline watched dumbly as she disappeared. Nick had driven Helen there, but he had not come in; he had not wanted to see her. That hurt, and she closed her eyes, the tears prickling under her lids.

The nurse came over and said, "In pain, Mrs. Storr? I'll get you something."

"Thank you," said Caroline, thinking, *not for this pain you won't*. There wasn't a painkiller in this world that could touch it.

IT WAS TWO DAYS before she saw Kelly, and even then the visit was a brief one. The nurse kept a wary eye on Kelly from a distance and Caroline wondered whether they were protecting her or their nice tidy hospital from a child's disturbing presence.

"When are you coming home, mummy? I got two gold stars for sums. You've got a scratch on your nose. Can I see your bandages? Do they give you your dinner in bed?" Kelly had a great deal to ask and to tell, and she poured it all out in her usual haphazard way, her eyes flying everywhere in open curiosity.

When Kelly allowed it, Caroline answered her, but she was concerned mainly with trying to read her daughter's small face, to work out whether Kelly was disturbed or not. Kelly was a vulnerable child. She had had too many shocks too early in her life, and Caroline knew she had to watch her and protect her from any more.

"I went to see a cartoon show at the pictures," Kelly said. "Auntie Hazel took me and I had raspberry-ripple ice cream and two Cokes. It was all dark in the pictures, but I wasn't scared."

Caroline swallowed. "Auntie Hazel?"

"She said I could call her 'auntie,' " Kelly said.

"Oh, did she?" Caroline had a slight sting in her voice. "When was this, Kelly?"

"Yesterday, after school, but I had my tea first because Uncle Nick didn't get home until five o'clock, and then we went."

"We?" Caroline said probingly.

"Uncle Nick, me and Aunt Hazel. In Uncle Nick's car, we went. Then we came home and Uncle Nick took Auntie Hazel out again and he said, 'Don't wait up for me,' only I woke up in the dark and he came and he wasn't even undressed, mummy."

Caroline stiffened, biting her inside lip. "Maybe he had just got home. What do you mean, you woke up? Did you have a bad dream, darling?"

"No," Kelly said thoughtfully. "Uncle Nick said it was the Cokes."

"Oh, I see," Caroline said, half smiling.

" 'Damn Cokes,' he said," Kelly expanded.

"Don't say 'damn,' darling."

"Uncle Nick says it; he says it all the time."

"He's a man," Caroline said.

"Auntie Hazel's silly," Kelly muttered with one eye on her mother.

"Why?" Caroline asked, knowing she ought to tell Kelly not to make personal remarks about grown-ups but dying to know what the child meant.

"She pretended to be scared in the cartoon when the witch came out of the wood and she made Uncle Nick hold her hand and kept squeaking. But I didn't, and she's silly!"

Mrs. Bentall had brought Kelly to the hospital in her small blue car. She had waited outside to give them some time alone, but now she appeared and said brightly that it was time to go. Kelly looked sulky and tried to climb on the bed, saying she wanted to stay. Caroline kissed her and promised she could come again soon, then gave her one of the apples Helen had brought her. Clutching it, Kelly was dragged away.

Mrs. Bentall smiled reassuringly at Caroline over her head as they left, but Caroline could not help wishing she could go, too. She was already very bored with hospital life and she did not like knowing that Kelly was waking up in the middle of the night. Next time Nick might not hear her and be on hand to make sure she was okay.

And what was he doing taking Kelly to see scary pictures with witches in them? Not to mention Hazel Skelton for company. Who needed a witch with her around, Caroline thought bitterly. How dared she tell Kelly to call her Auntie Hazel?

"When can I go home?" she asked the doctor when he did his rounds, a thin-faced nurse at his elbow.

"When I tell you," he said happily, grinning.

Caroline eyed him. "When will that be?"

"When I think you're ready," he said, grinning again. Then he walked away with the nurse, who gave her a dry look as if she felt Caroline had got what she'd asked for.

Frey wasn't much more help. "Why the hurry? Don't you like it here? A comfortable bed, good food...."

"Good food? You've got to be joking!"

"What's wrong with it?"

"Nothing a good cook couldn't cure," she agreed.

"You're having a holiday—can't you look at it like that?" asked Frey.

"Have I any choice?" she asked bitterly.

When she did go home at last it was in an ambulance, and she was under strict instructions to stay in bed until further notice. That was no hardship, she had to admit to herself. Her ribs were extraordinarily painful and she would need a cane to help her get around when she did get up because her ankle was in a cast and likely to remain in it for some time.

Kelly was beside herself with excitement. She sat on the bed talking after school that afternoon, giving Caroline a blow-by-blow account of her day. Helen sat in a chair next to them, listening and sewing, now and then grinning at Caroline at something Kelly had blurted out. Kelly's new school had at first found no favor in her eyes, but as she made friends and adjusted to the new environment she was beginning to forget Sharon and Miss Oldham and her big London primary school. Kelly had discovered that it was fun going to a school with smaller classes, where nature study meant going for a walk on the moors to pick heather and hope to catch a sight of rabbits and wild birds.

"You're looking tired," Helen said, getting up. "Time Kelly had her tea."

Vigorously protesting, Kelly was removed, and Caroline lay back with her eyes shut. Helen was right: she was tired. Kelly could be very tiring, much as she loved her. Even in good health, energy was needed to cope with a lively seven-year-old.

Drifting on the edge of sleep, she heard the door creak and lazily opened her eyes to glance across the room. Nick leaned against the doorway, his black hair shining with rain, the planes of his face taut and aggressive. Her heart turned over inside her, and she caught back a deep sigh.

"Awake?" He sounded brusque, which was his normal state when he saw her.

She nodded, struggling to sit up, and he strode across the room, saying sharply, "I'll do that."

Her breath caught in her throat as he bent over her. He smelled of wind and rain, and as his arm slid under her to lift her she was suddenly far too close to him, his hard cheek an inch or so from her own, and she was unable to stop herself from trembling.

He felt the betraying movement and stiffened, his body rigid. Still holding her, he turned his head to look into her eyes. Caroline's mind went hazy. They stared at each other for a few seconds while her whole nervous system jangled violently like a fire alarm gone crazy.

"Why didn't you tell me?" Nick said in a low deep voice, and she was so intent on struggling with her own wild sensations that she didn't have a clue what he was talking about.

"Tell you?" The question came huskily, her face blank.

"About Peter," he said, and now his voice had the rough edge of anger in it, and she took a long breath.

He didn't wait for her to answer. "Why didn't you tell me he was an alcoholic?" he demanded, and Caroline's pallor intensified.

"How did you find out? Helen?"

"She told me things that made my hair stand on end," Nick said rapidly in a terse voice. "Why couldn't you have told me?" The hand he had around her waist tightened, and she drew a painful breath.

"You're hurting."

"Sorry," he muttered, and lowered her against the banked-up pillows.

Nick sat down on the edge of the bed, his black head bent. "How could you let me go on thinking you were—"

Red coins burned in her cheeks. She broke in hurriedly, "Why did Helen tell you?"

"I made her," he admitted curtly.

"You shouldn't have," Caroline said, frowning. Poor Helen—had he browbeaten her into telling him the whole painful story?

"I had to know," Nick broke out hoarsely. He

looked up and the blue eyes were fixed and dark with emotion. "When you were delirious the night I found you on the moors, you kept on talking; you wouldn't stop. It didn't make sense at first. I couldn't grasp what it was you were saying—you had it all mixed up—and then light began to dawn, and I was so mad I wanted to break everything in sight. I sat there listening to you and I don't know how I stayed sane."

Caroline watched his profile as he looked away across the room. "It must have been a shock for you," she said gently.

"A shock!" His mouth tightened. "Couldn't one of you have told me the truth? I can understand Helen's wanting it kept quiet, but couldn't she have trusted me? Did she think I'd rush around Skeldale spreading it to everyone I knew? I've known her all my life! How could she keep me in the dark?"

"She was ashamed."

"God knows she had cause," Nick muttered. "I thought I knew Peter. I never knew him at all, did I? I was really taken in."

"How could you have guessed?" Caroline asked him in a quiet voice.

"Caroline," he said, his hand closing over one of hers, his fingers icy cold and tense. "I'm sorry. Why didn't you tell me? How could you let me go on behaving like a heel, crucifying you when all it needed was one word from you—"

"You wouldn't have believed me," Caroline said dryly.

His face darkened with angry color. "I...." He broke off, turning his head away so that she could no longer see his face. "No," he said heavily. "You're right, of course. I wouldn't have believed you."

There was a long silence. He removed his hand and pushed it shakily through his thick black hair.

"Helen says Forrester knew all the time."

She nodded, and he shot her a look from under his lashes, a frown appearing on his face.

"You went for help to him, not me," he said harshly.

"Frey got to know about it by accident; I didn't tell him," Caroline said in a wary little voice. How much had Helen told him?

Everything, it seemed. Nick swore thickly, shifting where he sat as though he wanted to do something violent.

"You mean, after Peter had beaten you up badly," he almost accused, turning the blue fire of his eyes on her.

She didn't answer, and his hands clenched into fists. "If I'd had any suspicion . . . !"

"He was sick," she said flatly.

"Sick!"

"Ask Frey—he'll explain," Caroline said with a sense of deep weariness. Nick was still angry, his long lean body pulsing with rage, and she was so tired of male violence. She wanted him to go. She wanted to be alone so that she could shut out the bad memories, the grief and fear and misery.

"I already did," Nick said. "I didn't buy it. Any man who could attack his wife and child like that—"

"He didn't know what he was doing. He turned nasty only when he was drunk."

"But he went on doing it!" Nick spat, his throat moving in a convulsive swallow. "He refused to give up drinking, Forrester said."

Caroline gave a long tired sigh. "He wouldn't admit he was an alcoholic," she said.

"If Forrester had had any sense he'd have informed the police of what was going on," Nick grated, his brows a heavy line across his forehead.

"Helen would have died of shame," Caroline said shortly.

"What about you?" Nick asked, staring at her. "And what about Kelly? How could Forrester let it go on happening? He told me himself that you were terrified."

"That's why I left," she said. "I had to get away before it got worse. I was afraid he might really harm Kelly. Each time he hit her he seemed more violent; he seemed to hate her."

Nick said something incoherent, his face rigid, then he got up and walked to the window and stood there staring out in silence for a while.

"Can you imagine how I felt when I found out?" he asked in a low voice. "How could you let me go on thinking about you like that when—"

"It doesn't matter," she said, and he stiffened.

"Doesn't matter!"

"I realized why you despised me. I couldn't tell you. I'd promised Helen I'd never tell a living soul. She was so afraid of all her friends knowing, of people talking—"

"But after he was dead," Nick interrupted. "What did it matter then?"

"When I got back here and found Helen so weak, what was I to do? I couldn't ask her to tell you then, and even if I had I still think you wouldn't have believed her. You'd have thought I had her fooled."

"You must have hated me," Nick said roughly.

"I understood," she said, and he looked around at her.

"Did you? Did you understand, Caroline?"

"Peter was your cousin. It was natural that you should believe him."

Nick watched her, his eyes probing her pale face. "And what I thought of you didn't matter one way or the other?"

She wasn't going to answer that question and he needn't think she was. She obstinately stayed silent, aware of his gaze but refusing to meet it now.

"Caroline," he began, and there was a tap at the door. Mrs. Bentall came in, smiling.

"Dr. Forrester's here," she said, and Frey followed her into the room.

Caroline gave a faint relieved sigh at the sight of him. He was so calm and steady, his gray eyes smiling as he glanced toward her.

"Hello, Caroline," he said in a warm voice, and Caroline held out her hand.

"Come in, Frey," she said eagerly.

Nick turned on his heel and walked out of the room without another word.

CHAPTER TEN

She saw nothing of him in the next few days. Caroline found that quite a relief. She did not have the energy, mental or physical, to cope with Nick in one of his more aggressive moods, and although he now knew the truth he had not seemed any more approachable in temper. Caroline almost got the feeling he still blamed her for something. Maybe he even blamed her because she had not told him the truth, despite the fact that he had admitted himself that he would not have believed it if it had not come out under harrowing circumstances. If he hadn't been certain that she was in delirium he would probably have thought she was trying to deceive him. Only her state of acute pain had convinced him.

She was allowed to come downstairs a week later. The bruises and grazes on her skin had largely healed and a good makeup covered what was left of them. Wearing a loose black caftan that could be draped over her plaster cast, she sat in the firelight with Helen and talked about Christmas, which was just a few days away.

The room was hung with gaudy tinsel, and swags of red-ribboned holly and ivy had been put up on the walls. The firelight flickered back from silver foil and a large gold star. The tall Christmas tree in the corner of the room glittered and gave off that resinous scent of pine. Under it were piled heaps of presents in bright wrappings. Helen said that Kelly could barely be persuaded to leave them alone.

"She keeps reading the labels and guessing what's in the parcels."

"I've finished wrapping all mine," Caroline said. It had passed the time pleasantly. The hours had dragged lately; her bedroom had been far too quiet and she had not found herself very charming company.

"What have you got for Nick?" Helen asked casually, and Caroline shrugged.

"Nothing very original. I had no idea what to get him. In the end I got him a book. You remember you picked up that pile of books for me last week? One of them was for Nick."

Helen looked dubious. "He doesn't read much fiction."

"This isn't fiction—it's a biography of Isambard Kingdom Brunel."

Helen looked blank. "Who's he?"

"He was an engineer. He built the first iron ship and designed iron railway bridges and a lot of other things—built railway tunnels and...." Caroline broke off, smiling as Helen looked at her with disbelief.

"I suppose Nick will be interested," Helen said, hardly bothering to hide her own total lack of interest.

"It was either that or a pair of gloves," Caroline said teasingly, laughing at her.

"He can always use a good pair of gloves," Helen said, and Caroline was amused.

"I'd noticed that when Nick did read a book it was nearly always either a textbook about engineering or a biography of some sort," she told Helen.

"You're very observant. I hadn't noticed him reading much at all."

Caroline looked away into the fire. "Oh, well," she said, hoping she hadn't flushed too revealingly.

The telephone rang and Mrs. Bentall came into the room to say the call was for Helen. Caroline sat alone looking at the flames as they crackled in the grate, their glare warming her face. Helen came back smiling.

"Would you mind if I went out this evening, dear? That was Janet. She wants me to go over to her place for a Christmas drink."

"I'll be fine," Caroline said at once. "I'll have to go back to bed early, anyway. You go and enjoy yourself."

"Sure?"

"Of course I'm sure," she said, shaking her head at Helen wryly. Then they both turned, smiling, as Kelly's voice was heard in the hall and she burst into the room, glowing like a peony after her drive back from school in the wintry afternoon.

"I got lots of cards and we had Father Christmas and he gave me a balloon and a toy watch." It was the last day of the school term. There had been a party that afternoon to which Kelly had been looking forward with great excitement. A large yellow balloon bobbed on a string she was clutching tightly in one hand as she kissed her mother.

One of the other mothers had brought her home,

and they heard the sound of the car throbbing away down the drive. Kelly ran to the window to wave to the little girl sitting in the back. "Emily's my favorite friend," she said, adding, "today." Kelly had a different favorite friend every day. She hadn't yet settled into any one particular group in the class.

"Have you still got your boots on, Kelly?" Mrs. Bentall asked sternly.

Kelly trailed out again, saying, "Oh, I forgot."

The door closed and Helen looked at the clock. "I think I'll run up and have a bath before I dress for the party. Do you know, I haven't been to a party for ages. I'm quite excited."

Left alone again, Caroline closed her eyes. She had been rather worried by her own lack of energy since the accident. Physically she knew she was much improved, but she seemed to feel tired all the time. Frey had reassured her. "It's cumulative, Caroline. You've been carrying a strain for years and when you had the accident it was the last straw. Both mind and body needed a long rest, but you weren't giving them one, so now they've got the perfect excuse and they're taking it."

She had laughed. "You make it sound as if they were conspiring against me."

"In a way I suppose they are," he'd said with amusement. "And I don't blame them. For the next few weeks I want you to take things easy. Don't even think. Just rest."

Easier said than done. How did you stop thinking? That would be a clever trick if she could only learn the knack.

Mrs. Bentall came into the room and Caroline jumped, her eyes flying open.

"What would you like for dinner, Mrs. Storr? Mr. Holt will be out tonight and so you're going to be on your own. I'll bring it up to you on a tray, shall I?"

"That's very kind," Caroline said wearily. Her tired feeling had abruptly deepened.

"What would you like?"

"I don't mind," Caroline said. "Anything will do." She had no appetite whatever and could not rouse any interest in the subject of food. For some unaccountable reason, she felt like crying.

Mrs. Bentall walked over to make up the fire, poking it vigorously. "Colder tonight," she said. "Snow up on the hills again. Shouldn't be surprised if we're in for a white Christmas."

"No," Caroline said.

"Mr. Holt did say that if the snow lays he'll make Kelly a toboggan; then she can go sledding down the hill at the back."

"She'll like that," Caroline said, her lids stinging with unshed tears. She asked casually, "Is he working late tonight?"

"No, not tonight for once," Mrs. Bentall said, straightening with a hand at her back, grimacing. "My lumbago's playing up again. I always get it when it's cold." She moved to the door slowly. "No, Mr. Holt's having dinner with that Hazel Skelton, saucy little madam that she is. I don't know what he sees in her."

The housekeeper shut the door and went out, and Caroline felt a tear slide down her face. She brushed it away angrily.

She heard Helen's voice later and hurriedly assumed a bright smile. She knew if Helen saw her looking depressed she would decide not to go to the party. As it was, Caroline had to work hard to persuade Helen to go.

"Are you sure? You look so pale," Helen said anxiously.

"I'm going to bed right now," Caroline assured her. "And I'm going to have my dinner in bed, Mrs. Bentall promises me, and then I'm going to go to sleep."

Helen laughed. "Bed's the best place to be in this weather." She kissed Caroline and left in the car of a friend who was also going to the party.

Kelly came and sat on the carpet and chattered to her mother until it was her own bedtime. "We're both going to bed," she said, giggling. "Isn't that funny?"

"Very funny," Caroline said with a smile that hurt. Mrs. Bentall helped her up the stairs and went back down to get the dinner. It arrived on a tray half an hour later, and Caroline forced herself to eat at least some of it. The strips of sole in a creamy sauce were delicious, but she did not feel hungry.

She had the light out by nine-thirty. She couldn't sleep. She lay in the darkness, tired and miserable, listening to the wind wail past the window and the clock in the hall ticking rhythmically. Her thoughts roamed aimlessly and in the end she switched on the bedside lamp and got out the paperback she had been reading. She forced herself to concentrate on it. It was a tense thriller, but Caroline was tense herself and the tension in the book had no effect on her. She read each word several times before she made sense of it.

Suddenly she heard footsteps on the stairs. For some reason they alarmed her. She reached out hurriedly to switch off the lamp and her hand caught the alarm clock and sent it crashing across the room.

Her door burst open and Nick launched himself into the room, his face taut.

"What's wrong?" he demanded, halting to look around the room. "What happened?"

"Sorry," she said nervously. "I dropped the clock."

He walked over to pick it up while she looked down, surveying him hungrily through her lowered lashes. He was wearing a dinner jacket, but he had undone his tie and loosened his collar. His hair had been brushed down flat, but as he put her clock back onto the bedside table he ran his hand through his hair and it sprang up, the vital black strands tingling with electricity. Caroline's pulse beat rapidly at her throat.

"How are you?" Nick asked, looking down at her.

"Fine," she said. "Absolutely fine." She gave him a bright false smile.

"Ankle less painful?"

She nodded.

"When does Forrester say the cast can come off?"

"Not for a while," Caroline murmured.

Nick pushed his hands into his pockets and stood by the bed, his attitude one of brooding intensity. "Came today, did he?"

She looked up at him. "No." She wished he would go. She could not bear to have him standing there so close. She was aware of him in every nerve.

"May I ask you a personal question?" Nick muttered, his eyes flicking to her face and away again.

"You may ask; you may not get an answer." Caroline stiffened as she waited for the question.

"Are you going to marry him?"

Pink flowed up her face. Her stomach plummeted. Nick focused on her, his black pupils very large in the blue brilliance of that stare. When she didn't answer immediately he said in a terse voice, "Are you?"

"As he hasn't asked me, I can't answer the question," Caroline managed to say in what she hoped sounded like a light and amused voice.

Nick drew a sharp breath. "All right, let me rephrase it. Are you in love with Forrester?"

Even more flushed, she said crossly, "How many personal questions do you plan to ask?"

"Give me an answer to that one and I won't ask any more," he said in a thick impeded voice.

"Why should I?" she demanded childishly, glaring at him.

He moved restlessly, his long body tense. "I have to know," he muttered.

"It's none of your business!"

His teeth came together and his nostrils flared in open fury. "Don't torture me, Caroline!"

She caught her breath, staring at him, doubting her ears. Had he really said that?

He swung away, his body moving in a restless uncertain way as if he didn't quite know what to do. With his back to her he said, "When he arrived the night I found you on the moors, you called him 'dear Frey,' you smiled at him and your face looked different. You don't look at me like that." He said the last sentence in a deep, almost sulky voice, emotion blurring the words.

"Don't I, Nick?" she asked, watching the way his hands were curled at his sides.

"For your sake I was relieved to see him arrive, but on my own account I could have happily seen him leaving for Timbuktu," Nick muttered.

"Poor Frey," she murmured, and he swung to look at her, his jawline taut, his eyes flashing.

"Are you? In love with him?"

Caroline couldn't even speak because her throat was dry and her body was trembling in the grip of a happiness she had never expected. Was she crazy? Was she indulging in wishful thinking? Or was that jealousy in his face, pain in his voice?

Nick stared at her fixedly. "Answer me, tell me, are you in love with Forrester?"

She sat very still, her heart beating so fast she wondered if he could hear it. "Why?" she asked huskily. "What has it got to do with you?"

"You know what it's got to do with me, Caroline," he said with a bitterness that darkened his face and voice. "I've made myself only too obvious, haven't I?" He looked at her, a stain of red washing up his face, his breathing audible in the quiet room.

"Have you?" she whispered uncertainly, looking back at him with hope and fear and wariness.

He moved as if he were on a string she was pulling, his lean body jerkily uncoordinated, and sat down on the edge of her bed to stare at her. His gaze drifted from her wide eyes to her mouth, and Caroline's pulses began to hammer violently.

His hand moved up to touch her hair, brushing it back from the pale outline of her face, his fingers lingering to run down the smooth skin of her cheek, trace the curve of her throat, the cool tips of them making her body tremble as though they left a trail of fire.

"Are you ever going to be able to forgive me?"

Dry mouthed, she looked down, listening to the beating of his heart as he shifted closer to her.

"Don't hate me, Caroline," he whispered, running his finger along the pink curve of her mouth. "I may deserve it, but don't. I behaved like a swine to you, but I was going through hell myself, don't you know that? Can't you imagine how it felt to want you so much I would have walked over hot coals to get you, yet to despise you from the bottom of my heart and loathe myself for the way I felt about you?"

She was trembling, so acutely aware of him that she could not meet his eyes in case he should see it.

"The more I saw of you after you came here to live, the more I found myself dizzy with uncertainty," Nick said. "I just couldn't understand you. At times I felt like a man on the wrong side of a mirror. Everything was distorted and out of key. I thought about you until it seemed my head would burst. You tormented me. I wanted you and I hated you and I was torn between the two. It's a marvel I didn't murder one of us."

"And most probably me," Caroline said, light-headed with joy and relief. "I was down in your book as a likely murder victim, wasn't I?"

Nick froze, staring at her, and she looked up then, very flushed, her eyes bright, her smile wavering.

"You were down in my book as the most desirable thing I'd ever set eyes on," Nick said huskily. His hand cupped her chin and he bent toward her, breathing faster. "Caroline...."

She put up a hand to block him, hold him off. "No," she said in a sharp voice, and Nick looked at her, his brows jerking together.

"No?" he asked in a stiff voice. "You don't want me?"

"I'm not sure exactly what your intentions are," Caroline informed him dryly. "I'd like more information on that, if you don't mind."

Nick's blue eyes sparked. "My intentions are strictly honorable," he said, and Caroline made a face.

"Oh, well, in that case, good night."

He looked stupefied. "What?"

"If you're proposing marriage I'd like more time to think about it," Caroline said sweetly. "After all, you have several obvious drawbacks as a husband. Your temper is appalling and you never believe a word I say without overwhelming proof that I'm telling the truth."

His wry grimace admitted the justice of that dig, then he eyed her speculatively, his brows lifting. "What if my intentions had been strictly dishonorable?"

"That would have been different," Caroline teased.

Nick's mouth curved upward. "In that case, may I reconsider my answer?"

"No," Caroline said. "I wouldn't hear of it. You've committed yourself now."

Nick laughed huskily, moving closer again. "Don't I even get one little kiss?"

She considered that. "One very little one," she conceded, offering him her cheek.

He bent forward as if to kiss it, then abruptly caught her head with one hand and turned it. His mouth met hers before she had notice of his intention and as the heated compulsion of his kiss closed over her lips she moaned with pleasure, flinging her arms up to close around his neck and clasp his black head between her hands. They kissed hungrily, Nick's fingers caressing her face all the time.

When he drew away his eyes were half-closed, his heart thudding next to her. "I love you," he whispered in a dry voice. "I love you desperately, Caroline."

She let her head fall onto his wide dark shoulder, her arms still curving around his neck. "Oh, Nick, darling, I've been in love with you for years. I couldn't bear it at times. Love's like a roller coaster, now high, now low, and I've been riding it so long I'm giddy."

"You and me both," he said, kissing her neck, his mouth moving so softly that a queer little shiver ran down her spine. "I've longed to do this, imagined doing it over and over again. Your neck is so smooth and pale and the scent of your skin drives me insane." He drew back and looked at her urgently, his eyes almost black with passion. "Marry me soon; I can't wait. I've waited so long already."

She smiled, her mouth unsteady. "I can't get married with one foot in a cast. We'll have to wait until Frey says the plaster can come off."

Nick's smile went. He looked down, his jawline grim. "Was there anything between you and Forrester, Caroline?"

She sat watching him. "No," she said flatly. "Do you believe me, Nick?"

He looked up, his eyes passionate. "Yes, I'll never doubt a single word you say again, my darling. I'll never forgive myself for the things I said to you, the way I treated you. After all you'd had to put up with from Peter, it's a wonder you didn't turn right off men."

"I did," she admitted, her face rueful. "But all the time I was in London I could never quite get you out of my head. You stuck there like a burr and I couldn't shake you off."

Nick moved restlessly, his face tense. "When I think how often I listened to Peter pouring out those lies about you. . . ."

"Don't talk about him," she said, her face disturbed.

"Does he still frighten you?" Nick asked, looking at her with sharp concerned eyes.

"Only when I remember," she said revealingly, and he made a low sound of anger under his breath.

"Oh, Caroline," he said. "When I think of what I put you through after all that—I hate myself."

"You're not allowed to," she said lightly. "You belong to me now and I won't have anyone hating you, even yourself."

He laughed and kissed her, stroking back her long honey-blond hair. Drowsily Caroline lay back on the pillows and Nick bent over her, his mouth warm and persuasive, his hand smoothly caressing her bare shoulder, her throat, the deep creamy valley between her breasts. Desire burned inside her. She felt the raging insistence of her own need growing by leaps and bounds. Nick sensed it, too, his passion flaring to meet hers, but suddenly they heard Helen's slow ascent of the stairs, a step at a time, and Nick shot upright, his face darkly flushed, his breath coming raggedly.

Caroline lay laughing, watching him teasingly as he stood up. There was a tap at the door. "Are you awake, dear?" Helen's face appeared and changed as she took in Nick's presence, his disheveled hair and flushed, self-conscious expression.

"Oh," Helen said, mouth rounding incredulously.

Nick uneasily shifted on his feet, pushing his hands into his pockets, his eyes not quite meeting Helen's disbelieving stare.

Caroline was tempted to laugh aloud, but she didn't. She looked at her mother-in-law with a smile of affection and coaxing. Helen wasn't going to know what to think. She'd had it all worked out: Caroline was going to marry Frey and they would all live happily ever after. Poor Helen. She looked as if she had been hit by a bus.

"Helen," Caroline said gently, "I've got something to tell you."

Harlequin Plus

THE BEAUTY OF YORKSHIRE

Yorkshire is the largest county in Britain, and its scenery is as varied as it is lovely: lonely stretches of mountainous moors, tranquil dales where quaint villages nestle, and a coastline that ranges in character from delightful sandy coves to huge rugged cliffs.

The Yorkshire dales are among the prettiest of England's sights, with their enchanting woods and meadows, their swift-flowing streams and rushing waterfalls. Dotted here and there with ancient churches, tiny villages and the ruins of old abbeys, the dales form an exquisitely peaceful region of the country.

The county centers on the city of York, one of the great medieval walled cities of Europe. York's three miles of walls have stood intact for six hundred years, and the massive York Minster, with its majestic towers and famous stained-glass windows, is the largest medieval cathedral in northern Europe.

Yorkshire is noted for industry, and its towns provide the world's finest woolens and worsteds. It also is famous for wayside inns serving York hams, fluffy Yorkshire puddings and rich brown parken, or gingerbread. And to millions it also means Brontë country. Here, in an old Georgian parsonage in the town of Haworth, the three Brontë sisters filled their tragically brief lives capturing the spirit of the windswept moorland in their classic novels of passion and rebellion.

SUPERROMANCE
SUBSCRIPTION
RESERVATION COUPON

 Complete and mail TODAY to

- -

Harlequin Reader Service

In the U.S.A.
1440 South Priest Drive
Tempe, AZ 85281

In Canada
649 Ontario Street
Stratford, Ontario N5A 6W2

Please reserve my subscription to the 2 NEW
SUPERROMANCES published every eight weeks
(12 a year). Every eight weeks I will receive
2 NEW SUPERROMANCES at the low price of
$2.50 each (total— $5). There are no shipping and
handling or any other hidden charges, and I am free
to cancel at any time after taking as many or
as few novels as I wish.

MY PRESENT SUBSCRIPTION NUMBER IS_____

NAME_____
(Please Print)

ADDRESS_____

CITY_____

STATE/PROV._____

ZIP/POSTAL CODE_____